BEACON HILL BOYS

KEN MOCHIZUKI

SCHOLASTIC PRESS
NEW YORK

LIBRARY OF CONGRESS CATALOGING-IN-PUBLICATION DATA
Mochizuki, Ken
Beacon Hill boys / by Ken Mochizuki. — 1st ed.   p.   cm.
Summary: In 1972 in Seattle, a teenager in a Japanese
American family struggles for his own identity, along with a group
of three friends who share his anger and confusion.
ISBN 0-439-26749-8
1. Japanese Americans — Juvenile fiction.   [1. Japanese
Americans — Fiction.   2. Individuality — Fiction.   3. Seattle
(Wash.) — History — 20th century — Fiction.]   I. Title.
PZ7.M71284Be   2002   [Fic]—dc21   2002002343

10 9 8 7 6 5 4 3 2   03   04   05   06

Printed in the U.S.A. 23 • First edition, November 2002
The display type was set in Pump Demi Bold and StreetVan-Haulinhouse
Solid. The text type was set in 12-point Sabon. Cover photograph © 2002
by Marc Tauss. Book design by David Caplan

"The responsibility of a writer is to excavate the experience of the people who produced him."

— James Baldwin

ACKNOWLEDGMENTS

My sincerest thanks to all who have read drafts of this story and offered valuable advice: Stephen Shoji, Peter Mizuki, Ron Chew, Gail Tremblay, Mayumi Tsutakawa, Nellie Fujii Anderson, Harriet Kashiwada; and especially Ed Sakamoto, who is largely responsible for me becoming a writer in the first place. My apologies to anyone I have inadvertently omitted during the twenty-one-year journey to publish this book.

And a special thanks to my editor Liz Szabla and agent Rosemary Stimola, who both believed in "The Boys" from the beginning, and saw the project through to the end.

I am also indebted to the founders and early leaders of Seattle's Asian American community, who paid the price for what they thought was right.

1. I tried to peek at what the waitress wore beneath her kimono as she leaned forward in front of me, serving the dishes of teriyaki beef, teriyaki chicken, teriyaki everything. I figured our waitress, with her high cheekbones, shiny black hair tied back, and just as shiny eyes, probably was around twenty-one.

And she busted me sneaking my peek.

But after she set the platters down, she glanced at me and grinned with a look that said, *You think you're the first to try that? And I* know *you won't be the last.*

I figured she thought I was too young for her, but that was okay with me. She could look at me any way she wanted to and still send me off to some serious fantasyland. Which was a whole lot better than where I was, listening to my family go on about me.

"Dan would rather keep that long hair of his instead of getting a haircut and looking for a job," my mom said as she reached for the food and began negotiating with my aunt over which way to pass the platters, right or left.

After they settled on a common direction, my aunt said, "You have to have a haircut to get a job anywhere these days. That's all there is to it." My aunt was a slightly altered version of my mom, sort of like the copy after a few carbon papers. Both had hair that took all day to curl with a ton of rollers, and curved black-frame glasses that went out of style a long time ago. *Hey, Mom and Aunt Margie,* I wanted to shout across the table, *this is 1972, not 1952.*

"Dan's more worried about his looks than he is about making a little money," Dad chipped in after slurping some tea. Dad was a natural to play the Japanese American version of one of those lecturing, all-American dads on TV — he had the slicked-back hair like them. "That's what's wrong with kids these days. They don't know how to swallow their pride and have a little character."

Tell me all about character, Dad. We had hiked a few blocks to this restaurant, instead of just parking across the street, because of my dad's showdown in the lot. Two cars squared off for the last remaining space. The other driver, the lady who looked like President Nixon's wife, waved some kind of ticket — it could've been any ol' piece of paper — like that gave her the right to the spot.

"What's she have in her hand?" Mom had asked.

"I dunno," Dad said. "But we better let her have that spot. We don't want any trouble."

So, my dad just smiled and waved that lady through. Mrs. Nixon and her passenger laughed at us as they turned into the final parking stall. . . .

Grandma always held her hand in front of her mouth as she chewed. She never said much, because she only spoke Japanese. My dad knew a lot, my mom knew a little; I didn't know a lick. My little brother, Steve, whose tenth birthday we were supposedly celebrating, stayed busy stuffing his face.

But then Grandma stopped eating for a second and looked up. Though her eyes seemed so far away behind thick glasses, I could swear she was giving me one of her *Hang in there* looks. She started saying something in Japanese. My dad ignored his mother, talking right over her.

"Now, here's a little bit of character for you," Dad said, nodding to my older brother, Brad, sitting at his side. I had heard the rest of this lecture more than enough times: Big Brother Brad, the big bad senior, bronze-skinned, square-jawed, and shorthaired, had a lot of character because he was clean-cut, had straight A's, was a baseball star, football star, and already knew he was headed to medical school. And my dad wouldn't mind having five like him —

"Then why don't you trade me in for another kid who has *character*?" I jumped in.

Dad pointed at me with his chopsticks. "Don't get smart. You've always had the potential. What I'm saying is some people use it a little more than others, you know?"

"Yeah, stupid," Brad tacked on as usual. "What do you and your reject friends call yourselves? 'Beacon Hill Boys'? Man, you guys are so corny."

Tell me about corny, brother Bradley. With your haircut, you're out of the same decade as Mom and Aunt Margie.

Steve said with his mouth full, "Yeah, maybe if I had another kind of brother, I would have two brothers who were *good* baseball players, instead of you. . . ."

I pummeled Steve on his thigh. "Man, shut up."

"Ow!"

"Hey! Knock it off!" Dad said.

"What are you getting mad at, Dan?" Mom interjected as she pushed her outdated glasses back up the bridge of her nose. "You don't really try, do you?"

"You just warm the bench," Steve added.

Dad bent forward a little and pointed behind him. "Yeah, he's always pulling slivers out of his rear end."

My family yucked it up real good.

Sure, guys, keep getting on my case and turn me into a juvenile delinquent. If that's what we're here for, you're all doing a good job.

Mrs. Oshima, a longtime friend of my parents, passed by our table. She and my mom went through the usual "How are you?" routine. My parents thought Mrs. Oshima and her old man were a big deal since they owned a Baskin-Robbins in town. Mrs. Oshima tried to prove my parents were right by wearing a fur coat.

Who's she tryin' to kid? Anybody knew wearing a fur coat around the end of March in Seattle was only for show.

"Come on, sit down and have something to eat," my mom said.

"No, no," Mrs. Oshima replied politely, "I'm meeting some friends here pretty soon. . . ."

Mom insisted. "That may take a little while yet, and you must be very hungry by now. Come, come . . . please sit down."

Mrs. Oshima repeated as politely as before, "No, really, I'm going to eat soon, anyway, but that's very kind of you to offer. . . ."

Mom pressed, "No, come, come sit down. There's plenty of food. . . ."

I wanted to scream: *She said "no" already! How many times you gotta hear it?*

"Well . . . all right. I'll have just a little while I'm waiting."

"Of course, might as well," Mom agreed. "I'm sorry we ordered only the cheapest dishes on the menu. That's us — not very high-tone at all. Hey, Dad, ask the waitress for another plate. Well, Dan, aren't you going to start passing her any of the dishes? I'm sorry for his lack of manners; you know kids these days."

She didn't even have a plate yet! *Jeeezz!* I didn't know how much more I could take. Mom wouldn't have anything to be sorry about if she didn't keep coming up with something to be sorry about!

"My, your boys are growing so fast," Mrs. Oshima gushed. "And your oldest boy here, he's going to some real smart-people's college, isn't he?"

"Stanford," my dad announced right away, and raised his teacup like he was making a toast. "Premed."

Mrs. Oshima gushed again. "My, your kids are so bright!"

The way Brad's face beamed, he could've brought in a 747 for a landing in the fog. He made me sick.

"How about your next oldest boy here?" Mrs. Oshima continued. "Is he going to do the same?"

Mom frantically gestured for us to pass all of the plates Mrs. Oshima's way, then said, "I don't know. Dan's too busy messing around, so he'll probably have to settle for a regular college like the University of Washington. It's *your* kids who are the really bright ones."

"No, no, not at all."

"Sure."

"No, no, no . . ."

Dad asked, "Say, Betty, are you looking for any help at your shop? Dan here is looking for a job."

"Well, I'll be sure to ask my husband. Dan would be just perfect working there, a nice, polite boy like him. But his hair needs a little trimming."

"That's what we're trying to tell him," Mom said as she thoroughly wiped her mouth after every bite. "But he just won't listen."

You better believe I'm not cuttin' my hair just to scoop those 31 flavors.

Mrs. Oshima's friends arrived, so she left our table. Of course, since she came to eat with them, she only took a few token nibbles out of the food on her plate — food we could've had instead.

My little brother's birthday dinner ended with at

least one piece of food remaining on every platter. Even if we were starving to death, no one would dare touch those last uneaten pieces. If you did, everyone would watch you clean the plate and think you were a pig.

My aunt hoisted one of those platters. "Here, pass this to Dan. He's a growing boy."

Sure, set me up, guys. I knew I was supposed to refuse it, but, hey, I didn't get enough to eat. All the leftovers started coming my way — a bucket brigade passing platters to dump all over Dan Inagaki.

As expected, everyone else sat there silent while they stared at me eating, making me feel as though I faced a firing squad.

If that was the case, couldn't they cut me a little slack while I finished my last request?

Man! *Where* did *this crazy way of acting come from?*

2.

If there had been a job that paid by the hour for sleeping, I would've been on my way to becoming a millionaire. As it was, the clock radio clicked on way too soon each morning. . . .

Still more asleep than awake, I heard some news about parents throwing rocks at school buses used to integrate the schools, and the U.S. bombing the hell out of North Vietnam. Then Marvin Gaye singing "What's Going On." Marvin's song was practically an anthem at our school — it was hip to be against the war and be for peace and helping out your brother man.

Apparently, singing along with Marvin was one thing, doing what he said was another.

At least I had a good year to go before I would have to register for the draft. Would the war still be going on by then? Some of the senior guys at school were pretty worried about being drafted, especially the ones who weren't getting that student deferment by going to college. But even if Uncle Sam changed his mind and everybody had to go, I knew Big Brother Brad would never end up in 'Nam. Guys like him never had to do anything they didn't want to do.

Getting ready for the day left me no choice but to look at myself in the mirror.

Not a pretty sight.

I ran a hand through my coarse black hair. It wasn't real long — I mean, I didn't look like a rock star or anything — but thick waves did cover my ears and crawl down most of my neck.

At least I didn't have to bother with my hair too much anymore. A few years before, I couldn't leave the house until I'd plowed creamy, white grease through that black mop. Brylcreem, the stuff was called. The TV ad claimed "a little dab will do ya." It showed us a James Bond–type dude in a hot Ping-Pong match with a fresh-off-the-boat–looking Asian guy. The hair on the Asian guy's bushy head flew all around; the white guy was cool because his hair stuck to his head like cement. The Asian guy slammed that Pong ball and won the match, but the white guy walked off with the fine Asian sister.

That's why I started using Brylcreem back then. Not that it helped. I never walked off with the fine Asian lady, or any lady, for that matter.

I looked again at my mess of hair, my flat nose, my pencil neck connected to a head too large for a lanky body.

Maybe Brad was right: I must've been adopted, since I didn't look like him.

If all that wasn't enough, the bad news continued: no girlfriend, no good at sports, my parents on my case for not having a job and not having stellar grades. In other words, *I wasn't living up to brother Brad.*

My mom's hard knuckles rapped on the bathroom door.

"Hurry up! You're going to be late! No wonder Brad leaves without you!"

Almost three more months of junior year, then a whole year more in that institution called high school. I didn't know which was worse: doing time at home, or at school — at the insane asylum, or the penitentiary.

The Beacon Hill neighborhood of south Seattle could have been one of those paint-by-number oil paintings. One-story wood houses with neat lawns were lined up behind towering maple trees that quietly shaded both sides of main streets. Strong, sprawling roots from those trees cracked and buckled concrete sidewalks. Robins and sparrows chirped away, not bothering to suspend conversation while passenger jets flying in and out of the Seattle airport rumbled noisily overhead.

This was still life for sure, with the pretty picture only occasionally marred by yards with wild dandelions and overgrown crabgrass aspiring skyward through spaces in graveyards of junk. Rusting car parts gave any kid a hands-on demonstration in oxidation, as did swing sets without swings, and a tricycle junior no longer parked inside.

Perfectly and predictably rectangular, Herbert Hoover High stood on a sloping side of Beacon Hill. It had a roof with white stone cornices maybe stately in another century but worn dull and dirty by decades of rain and freeway exhaust. Tangled, twisting ivy and splotches of green moss crept over brick that had blackened with mildew and decay. From upper-story windows, bored students could gaze at more and more freeways being built in the valley below. Down there, The Boeing Company also built bigger and bigger planes.

Since Hoover was in south Seattle, it was a South End school. Hoover's entire student body would equal the size of one class in a North End school. Those almost-all-white North End schools had swimming pools and closed-circuit TV studios; we were lucky if our school could scrounge up a film projector. For lunch, we ate what the kids at rich North End schools didn't — made into a meal and reheated in an aluminum tray, TV-dinner style.

Each day as I walked down more scuffed linoleum floors and around more mud brown walls, I also passed the student body of Hoover High: a third black, a third white, a third Asian — the way it had always been at every school on Beacon Hill. There were a lot of Afros and long, straight hair; a lot of army jackets, white T-shirts, and bell-bottom jeans or Levi's with hems whacked off and frayed. No need for forced busing at Hoover — equality had been achieved. We were all oppressed equally just by being students at that school.

And Hoover was even more of a drag than other South End schools. Hoover's student body came from The Hill or surrounding industrial areas, so most of the dads worked at Boeing. Our rival school at the bottom of the other side of The Hill was Andrew Jackson High, where rich students from swanky neighborhoods around Lake Washington mixed with poor and tough inner-city kids. A couple of years earlier, when a black kid at Jackson got beat up by some white guys, the Black Panthers showed up. Wearing their black berets and armed with bullhorns, they took over the school until the cops came and teargassed everybody out.

Nothing exciting like that would ever happen at Hoover. Turmoil and progress might have swirled around The Hill, but Hoover stagnated in a still pond.

The bell clanged, ending another day at the penitentiary, and I headed toward the gym to get ready for a baseball game. Overhead in the hall, a fluorescent light crackled and blinked. Those bulbs always bugged me when they busted. Hoover had a lot of those — the kind that just couldn't go off and stay off when they'd had it. They just had to flicker away, letting the world know *I'm dying! I'm dying!*

I looked up and thought, *You ain't the only one having to eat it these days, brother man.*

Behind me, I heard some hard leather heels hitting the hallway floor. "Hey, Dan, what's happenin', man?"

Eddie Kanegae grinned and slapped me five. He was decked out as usual in his gray fedora "brim" hat, black leather jacket, black high-heel boots, and polyester flared slacks with hems almost dragging on the ground. Eddie always complained how hard it was for small guys to find cool clothes. Eddie's getups looked more like costumes than clothes. Thick strips of hair jutting down each cheek compensated for the sideburns he couldn't grow. Eddie was also on the baseball team and headed to the gym with me.

"Yeah, man," Eddie said as he strutted down the hall, clutching the handle of his alto sax case, "I'd rather be jammin' with the brothers in the band room, but, you know the deal — we gots to play us some ball so we can get out of gym class."

"Yeah," I chuckled, "I heard that."

Eddie sure had guts — no one else at Hoover tried so hard to be black. He had the rich older brother living on Mercer Island, the Shangri-la of suburban Seattle. Eddie's sisters were teachers, studying to become principals. Eddie, the youngest, was supposed to follow suit as a success story, so his parents jumped all over his case for trying to get in a band. While I had only one older sibling to be constantly compared with, Eddie had three. Which meant Eddie got three times more hassle from his parents than I did.

Music was just something to listen to while working — it could never *be* work, his parents told him. How would it look with a bum in the family who didn't have a *real* job? And they scolded him about his black trip — that he was embarrassing himself and the Kanegaes, that no good would come out of trying to be like *them*.

But I could understand Eddie's trip — it wasn't like us Asian guys made the cool music. We couldn't dance; we didn't set the trends with the threads. We couldn't say anything loud like "I'm black and I'm proud."

Us Asians, we had nothing cool we could call our own. In fact, we were just getting used to calling ourselves "Asians" instead of "Orientals" like our parents did. And just being good kids with good grades so we could grow up to be like our good brothers and sisters didn't cut it as cool anymore. . . .

Eddie and I walked outside to get to the gym. We both checked out the overcast sky. Typical. I once saw a bumper sticker that summed up Seattle pretty well: THE SEATTLE RAIN FESTIVAL — OCTOBER THROUGH JUNE. That "festival" kept grass green, lakes blue, and forests growing in backyards. So, if Seattle was one big park, why wasn't I having any fun?

"Looks like we could get rained out," Eddie said.

As gravity pulled me and Eddie down the stairwell, Eddie's heels created a racket that sounded like he was tap dancing his way down to the gym. Inside the locker room, cleats clattered and lockers banged open and shut. Under more glaring fluorescent lights, guys ran around in jockstraps and we were hit by the inevitable smell of Ben-Gay and armpit sweat.

Frank Ishimoto sat on one of the long, varnished benches in front of a row of lockers. I had known Frank forever, even longer than Eddie; we had all grown up on Beacon Hill and had gone to the same schools. Through no fault of his own, Frank wore an invisible "D" on his chest. His parents had committed the Japanese American unthinkable: They got divorced. What kind of image was that to project to the rest of America? And to my parents' generation, kids of divorced parents were damaged goods.

Already suited up, Frank repeatedly punched his chubby fist into his mitt, rounding out the palm. His year-round, part-time gig at a gas station put permanent grease stains into every crease on his hands. And a baseball uniform sure wasn't meant to flatter a squat, pudgy body like his. Frank tried to be with it and grow his hair long, but those sleek black strands fell limply over the sides of his bowling-ball head. Old horn-rim glasses secured by an elastic band didn't help, either, but Frank couldn't risk breaking his good aviator wire-rims on the field.

"Hey, Frank," I said as I sat down next to him, "how many balls you gonna catch today?"

"Yeah," Eddie added, "and how many home runs you gonna hit?"

"Man, you guys," Frank replied as he punched into his mitt harder, "you know we probably won't even get to play."

"Yeah, ain't that the truth?" Eddie and I said in

sync. Anybody who turned out for baseball at Hoover made the team. Playing school sports substituted for PE. For the three of us, riding the baseball bench still beat running laps on the track in gym class.

I dialed the combination on my locker. At the top of that flimsy metal locker door, written in black felt marker on masking tape, was INAGAKI — the name nobody bothered to pronounce right. "In-gawk-ee" remained standard fare; sometimes I was just plain "Gawky."

Then I heard some palms slapping five, someone getting respect from the rest of the team. "Hey, Bradley 'I,' what's happenin', man?"

Big Brother Brad showed up at our row of lockers — "The Man with the Golden Arm," the team's ace pitcher, the school's star quarterback, the son and brother my family wished they had another one of instead of me. He hated our last name, so he just went by the initial. Took too long to say, and nobody could say it right, anyway, he claimed.

"Hey, guys," Brad said, deigning to recognize the existence of Frank and Eddie. He stuffed his physics and calculus books into the top shelf of a locker near the end of the bench.

"Hey, Brad," Frank and Eddie replied, deigning to recognize Brad's existence in return.

Brad's letterman's jacket had so many gold stars, bars, and sports symbols sewn on the letter, hardly any red felt of the "H" showed through. That was a ritual after every school quarter: my mom in the living room sewing something new on Brad's jacket. He started undressing, flashing all that sculpted sinew and bronze skin — I couldn't remember him looking any other way.

Brad said to me, Eddie, and Frank: "You know, if you guys could quit moping around together, you'd probably be playing today."

Sure, Big Brother, easy for you to say.

Since the beginning of his senior year, Brad had been hanging out after school in the North End. He'd met his girlfriend there, at an away-game. Christine Holter. Tall, blond, long-legged.

And white. He liked to show her off at the games.

She was fine, all right.

Brad told teachers there was nothing wrong with being called "Oriental" when a lot of Japanese, Chinese, and Filipino students I knew at Hoover were fighting for "Asian." He didn't mind being called a "Jap" in the North End if that meant he could hang out with his girlfriend's friends. On Beacon Hill, the "Asians" like Eddie, Frank, and me had another name for him: a Banana. Yellow on the outside, white on the inside.

19

Yeah, we could knock my brother all we wanted. But I had to admit: Any guy would want his smarts, his athleticism — his girlfriend!

But did we have to be *him* to get all that?

Suddenly, the locker room was infused with Donny Hathaway's jazzy version of "What's Going On." Hearing the latest soul jams always announced the arrival of Jerry Ito. When we were little kids . . . whenever I or Frank or Eddie or anybody on The Hill got called a "Jap," we brought Jerry along the next time. Then we weren't called names anymore. We all grew up attending the same Methodist church on Beacon Hill; Jerry was the only guy we ever knew who got kicked out of Sunday school.

Jerry's wavy, uncombed hair fell almost to his shoulders and often over piercing eyes you didn't want piercing into you. A loose, white T-shirt hid a bulky torso; his thighs strained his jeans at the seams. One hand seemed perpetually balled into a fist, and the other clutched a cassette player forever blaring hip R&B.

Since Jerry had no problem throwing people around, he was a natural for wrestling and playing defensive end in football. But no such sport existed during the spring, so track would have to do. Only Jerry could run the sprint events, then throw the shot put in between. Coaches didn't try hard to coach him — they just turned him loose. And as Eddie, Frank, and I knew, his mom and dad did the same.

When we were younger, his parents and other Japanese American neighbors tried to make Jerry a good kid like their kids — they tried to be extra patient with him, tried to teach him that all obstacles and problems in life didn't have to be overcome with brute force. Jerry threw people for a loop: "What? A Japanese American *bad* boy?" So, Jerry decided early on that, if he had already been branded as The Bad Boy, it took less effort to excel at being bad than to reform and fit in.

I guess with six kids in the family, Jerry's parents figured they could cut their losses, and Jerry was jettisoned as a loss. He still lived at home, but his folks dealt with him as they did with anything unpleasant: Ignore it, and hope it goes away. Dads on The Hill told their kids — especially their daughters — to stay clear of that Ito boy who marred the image of the nice, quiet, studious Oriental.

Brad yelled over to the track bench, "Hey, Ito, turn that down. Guys here are trying to get ready for their game."

Brad thought he could tell anybody what to do since he *was* "The Man with the Golden Arm."

Jerry sat down and straddled a bench. "What's that, Uncle Tom . . . I mean Banana Brad . . . I mean, Bradley?"

Brad glared at Jerry something fierce; Jerry countered with a *So, what?* smirk as he flicked up the volume a few numbers. Jerry stuck up two fingers instead of his customary one. "Peace, brother. . . ."

The track coach walked by. "Hey, Ito, cut the music and get suited up." Jerry glanced at me, Eddie, and Frank as he punched his tape machine off. If an alligator could grin, that's the look he gave us right then: Messing up Brad was all in a day's work. Other than athletics, he had to have pride in something.

Everyone knew when Coach Hyde walked in, because his mood at the moment — either good or bad — traveled instantly over the airwaves. With his long sideburns, glassy green eyes, and chest hairs up to his neck, Coach Hyde looked like he fancied himself more fit for the French Riviera than Beacon Hill.

Coach ambled past Brad, punched him playfully on the shoulder, chomped his gum loudly, and said, "Hey, Bradley, those fast hands you got do you any good at the drive-in movie?"

Brad just grinned. "Hey, Can-guy!" Coach shouted down the row of lockers. "Gettin' any action besides that picture in your locker?"

Just like my name, Eddie's was also fair game to be butchered. One of the black guys, a starter, with his baseball cap stuffing down a big Afro, chimed in, "C'mon, Can-guy, Coach wants to see that nasty business you're hidin'."

Coach laughed with the team, one of the guys.

Poor Eddie looked stunned as he stood in front of his locker, his face flushed as if he had just been busted for peeping in the girls' locker room. "Oh, man, why's everybody on my case?" Eddie said, tugging the bill on his cap.

"C'mon, let's see it," Coach ordered.

Eddie nervously swung his locker door open, revealing a glossy magazine centerfold neatly taped to the inside.

"Man, check it out. . . . Eddie can't even wait till he gets home," one of the white starters quipped, sending a ripple of cackles through the team.

Coach pushed his cap back on his head and let loose a low whistle. "Hey, Bradley, is that the bod your honey's got? Guess only you are lucky enough to know. Most Oriental guys just dream about something like *that*. You know *Can*-guy does at night."

The entire team chuckled, whether they wanted to or not, because we were supposed to do everything as a team. Of course, Brad laughed along with the coach.

23

I didn't when I saw Eddie just watching everybody as he slowly swiveled his locker door back and forth.

Coach never did — and he never would, I'd bet — make a crack like that about one of the black guys.

A metallic *bang* shot through the room, making us all jump. Eddie slammed his locker door shut, opened it, and slammed it again and again, each slam a deafening crash. The baseball guys sitting around Eddie leaped like flies taking off. Shocked at first, some of the guys began to laugh harder at him.

I remember a time when Eddie just took it, when he was pushed into his locker and locked in; when at a party in junior high, he was put up to slow dance with the tallest girl in the class. During those days, he thought his solution was to dangle from a chin-up bar for a while, said daily stretching would make him taller. As time went on he realized other aspects about himself, his face, his name, figured into the persecution, too. By the time we were in high school, Eddie fought back the only way he could: If he was forced to go onstage, he was going to finish the show. If people were going to laugh at him, he was going to make them laugh until it hurt.

But the way Eddie was losing it, I figured I had better calm him down.

"Hey, Eddie," I said, loud enough so he could hear me. "Be cool, man. It's just a game. . . ."

"Man, shut up," Brad said to me, with a foot on the bench as he knotted one of his shoes. "Can-guy's tryin' to psych himself up. Maybe he wants to be a winner! Not like some people . . ."

Brad turned to Eddie. "C'mon, short boy, when you gonna grow up?"

Eddie banged that door fast and furious.

"Still buyin' your clothes at the boys' department?"

Faster and harder yet.

Frank shook his head and whispered to me, "Brad sure is cold-blooded!"

But, for Brad, winning had always meant more than feelings. "Look at that loser! He's nothin' but a little chump! He's nothin' but a quitter!"

His face raging red, Eddie snatched a grungy wet towel off the ground, balled it up, wound up, and heaved, pitching a fastball. The towel slammed against a locker, rattled a whole row of combination locks, and dropped DOA to the concrete floor. Eddie thrust his fists in the air and screamed, "Let's kick butt!"

"Yeah!" the team agreed, still laughing. I didn't laugh, and Frank had sat there the whole time as if he were watching TV coverage of some bad disaster.

"You see that?" Coach could barely get out as he cracked up. "That there is a winning attitude. Can-guy is learning what a winning attitude is. Bradley 'I' *knows* what a winning attitude is. Looks like he needs to teach little 'I' what it is."

It was my turn for everyone to stare and smirk. Coach wrapped an arm around Brad's shoulders and led him and the team out to a waiting bus, Eddie jogging behind. Frank and I pulled up the rear. I figured the three of us might get to play if our team was leading by, say, ten runs. The baseball team filed through one door of the gym, the track team out another. While the track guys all wore their matching crimson sweats, Jerry had on the pants, but just a white T-shirt over his jersey. While the rest carried their matching red and white vinyl bags, Jerry had all he needed: his cassette machine, and his track shoes tied together and slung around his neck.

"Hey, pretty good show, Eddie," he said. "Hey, boys," Jerry said to me, Frank, and Eddie, "I might have a little somethin' for you guys . . . for all your pain and sufferin' 'cause you ain't like your hero, Bradley 'I.' "

"Yeah . . . right," Frank answered sarcastically, tossing his mitt into the air, tumbling end over end. "We wanna be like Dan's brother when we grow up."

Eddie uttered an as-if-we-didn't-know chuckle and

said, "So, Jerry, is what you got gonna make our pain and sufferin' go up in smoke?"

Jerry grinned his alligator grin. "Hey, boys, what you don't know won't hurt you."

That was easy for Jerry to say. He didn't have anything to lose, while the rest of us had to worry about the future, about life after high school, about something called college. . . .

Besides, if Brad ever found out I was trying any of that, he would tell my parents, and kick my butt. Not necessarily in that order.

"Well, whatever you got, Jer, lay it on us anytime," Eddie said as if he were already an established veteran. "I mean, *aaanny-tiiime.*"

Anything . . . anytime . . . if only it were so easy. I'd known Frank, Eddie, and Jerry almost all my life, and come to think of it, I couldn't remember a time when we weren't searching for someplace where we would be somebodies, where our families weren't constantly on our cases, where we would be given credit for what we *could* do, rather than endlessly criticized for what we couldn't.

Beacon Hill was the only place we knew, but I was beginning to seriously doubt whether it would ever be the place where any of us would look forward to waking up. And be happy with what we saw in the mirror.

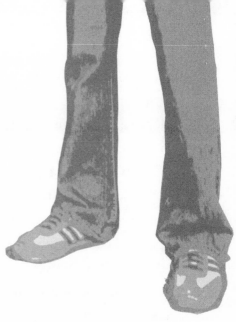

3. Before the start of the first class-period of the next day, I turned into the Student Activity Center — the SAC — for my "study" period. The SAC was supposed to be the center for school spirit, the meeting room for cheerleaders, school clubs, and student government. But it really was just a hangout — the first place teachers looked to find students skipping class.

That morning, the sun actually stuck around and warmed the long room, its rays liberating a musty odor from the worn hardwood floor. I wished my wrists were taped or my legs hurt so bad I had to hobble around because I had done my crucial, clutch-play bit in securing The Win. But I hadn't even had to shower after yesterday's game.

I was usually the first one in the SAC. I worked it that way so I could pick my spot for the best view. But, that day, my subject had arrived before me.

"Hi, Dan."

There she was. Alone.

Janet Ishino greeted me in that smooth way she talked, drawing out the sound of each word to make them last. She set her purse and books on one of the clunky pinewood tables in the center of the room and sat down, a sunbeam lighting her hair from behind. Black hair almost brown fell around her shoulders in loose curls, framing her eyes, dark eyes that seemed to reflect stars even during the day — the same as my favorite movie star, Natalie Wood.

Oh, man. . . .

I tried to think fast — of something I could talk to her about so I could hover around her, buy some time.

C'mon, Inagaki, it doesn't have to be the Gettysburg Address!

"Hi."

And then what did I do? I retreated to a table at the other side of the room as the SAC regulars sauntered in: football players and their cheerleader girlfriends; freckle-faced guys who were baseball stars; stoners with the longest hair in school; guys with cars with beer in the trunk. In less than a minute, Janet found herself surrounded by guys — guys who beat me in a race I didn't have the guts to enter. Black, white, Asian — they were all united by the same hormones flowing faster than Niagara Falls.

I sat at that table crammed into a corner, my back against the wall, legs bent, my arms wrapped around the knees of my faded Levi's. The only subject I wanted to study sat before me.

Janet was going to graduate among the Top Ten in her class, along with Brad. One of her accomplishments at school, among many, was being president of HHEX — Hoover High Exchange. When students from other schools came to Hoover, she showed them around, talking up how great Hoover was. Which, as far as I was concerned, made her a great actress on top of everything else. She could talk easily with anybody — something I could never do. And, of course, guys wanted to visit Hoover once they knew she led the tour. No wonder she was headed to UCLA in the fall, to Southern California, the glitz, showbiz, Hollywood. UCLA was definitely her kind of school.

Janet leaned back and laughed at someone's joke, so at ease with all the attention. She ran her fingers through her hair as it fanned out across her white sweater; she crossed her long legs that looked even longer because of the lavender miniskirt she wore.

"Oh, my God!" I uttered, then immediately clamped a hand over my mouth. *Man, did I really say that out loud?* Not that it would have mattered, since I just snatched the very words from all the guys ringed around her. Again I settled for watching her from a distance, storing the image with all the others that had piled up since I first saw her four years ago in eighth grade.

Leaning over Janet's table, propped on his elbows and closest to her, was Davie Miles, senior semi-star running back on the football team that partied as though they won the Rose Bowl if they won just one game. Wearing his trademark train engineer's cap, he had his cake-cutter comb stuck through the Afro bulging out of the back of his head.

On the other side of Janet sat Davie's backfield teammate, his quarterback, Big Brother Brad. The papers proclaimed Brad as the quarterback who never lost games — it was his team that could hardly win. He was having more success as a pitcher since the baseball team was better. Slouched in his chair in his letterman's jacket, Brad was trying to look bored. And not succeeding. Even though he'd told me that he never hit on Janet because he "wasn't into Oriental girls," I knew it was because Janet was the one person Brad couldn't impress. And that aspect about her impressed me even more.

"Hey, Dan, what'choo starin' at?"

Eddie had just walked into the SAC and followed my gaze. "Oh, man!" Eddie said to himself when he saw Janet, too. "Lord have mercy on us all *to-day*!"

Davie said something to just Janet that made her smile.

Then Frank trudged in.

"Hey, what's happenin', Frank?" Eddie and I asked, as always.

"Man, you know the answer to that," Frank grumbled back same as any other day. He paused by us, surveying the room, then headed to the group around Janet. Since Janet's performance was SRO, Frank stood on the fringe. I cringed as I watched him, my chin on my knees. Frank looked like he was window-shopping, gazing at the dream, whether Janet or that clique of cool. He laughed along with everyone else, but did he know what everyone was laughing about?

Frank circled the room and ended back where he started. With us.

"Hey, Can-guy!" a baseball teammate called out from across the room. "What's this?" He imitated Eddie slamming his locker door. "Blam! Blam! Blam! Blam! Blam!"

The crowd chuckled.

Eddie slid his brim over his face. "Oh, man!" he said for all to hear. The cool crowd laughed again.

The study period continued to tick away before I would have to go to some real classes. Eddie kept his brim low on his forehead as he wiggled his fingers in the air, rocking to some soul song in his mind as he played his air sax. Frank found a chair and slept sitting up. I tried to read more of *A Clockwork Orange* for a report I had to do for language arts. In that book, whenever a gang of futuristic hoods who called themselves "Droogs" thought something was really cool, the biggest and the baddest, they declared it as being "real horrorshow." As in they beat up somebody "real horrorshow."

But how could I read and stare at Janet at the same time? That is, until she dropped the atomic bomb. Real horrorshow.

"I wish there were more people in my health class," Janet said, I thought for the sake of conversation. That class mixed juniors with seniors.

"Who's in it?" Brad asked.

Janet listed off a few names. ". . . your brother's in there, and Frank's in there," she said, nodding in our direction. "But there's nobody in there —"

Janet tried to cut through all the "oooh's" and laughter, waving her hands in the air, trying to flag everyone down. "That's not what I meant." Then she stared straight at me and seemed to reel in what she had just said. "I mean, nobody I can really talk to, anyway —"

But the second half of her indictment got lost in the horrorshow blast of the first.

"Oh, man, that's *cold*!" Eddie mumbled, pulling the brim of his fedora over his face again. Brad looked at me and laughed.

Nobody, huh?

Frank apparently wasn't asleep. He scooped up his books and waited till he felt sure the cool crowd had preoccupied themselves with themselves again. Then he made his move, zipping past me and Eddie and stepping quickly out of the room without a sound. No one noticed he had left. Frank did that often, and he was good at it.

"*Heeeeey*, Frank! Where you goin'?" a voice boomed in the hallway.

Jerry Ito sounded stoned. He cruised into the SAC with his music machine playing Billy Preston's "Outa-Space."

"Whadda you guys lookin' at?" he said to me and Eddie. Jerry stared for a few seconds at Janet and the guys around her and said, "How much you guys wanna bet I can hustle her right now?"

"Right now?" Eddie asked like Jerry was out of his mind and knowing Jerry probably was.

"Right now."

"What's the bet?"

"If I do this, you hafta cop some of my smokes."

"Okay," Eddie said, shooting me a nervous grin. "You're on, brother man."

Jerry left his deck on our table; his footsteps made no sound as he approached Janet. With his hands clasped behind his back, he acted all innocent. . . .

"Hey, Ito," Davie Miles said, and laughed, "what-'choo up to, man?"

. . . as he sneaked up and reached around, squeezing Janet from behind in a big bear hug.

"What kind of caveman stuff is that, Ito?" Brad said.

Janet glanced up, surprised. "Jerry Ito? What do you think you're doing?" She seemed more shocked than irritated.

"Forget you, then," Jerry muttered loud enough to be heard. And the way Jerry shot a glance at Brad, Eddie and I knew Jerry pulled up just short of pounding Brad one. Jerry headed back our way, snatched up his sound machine, then ambled toward a red vinyl couch unusually unoccupied as some student typically slept there through study period. Jerry set his cassette player on the floor, plopped onto the sofa with a slapping thud, and threw his jacket over his head. "Outa-Space" jammed on.

Brad said from halfway across the room, "Hey, Ito, if you're gonna just go to sleep, why don't you turn your machine off, too."

"Brad," Davie Miles said, trying to keep the peace, "it's okay, man. . . ."

Jerry lay motionless, his coat over his face.

Brad stopped rocking in his chair and shoved it back, sprang up, and maneuvered through the gaggle of guys to where Jerry lay. "Not everybody likes what you listen to, Ito." Brad stooped down to Jerry's cassette machine.

"Don't touch it," Jerry said, his voice muffled beneath his jacket.

"C'mon, man," Brad said. "You're not the only one in here, you know."

"I said, don't touch it!" Jerry said louder through his jacket.

Brad hit the STOP button. *Clack.* Nobody in the SAC was talking anymore.

Jerry's fist and arm rocketed straight up and punched his jacket off his face, shooting the coat across the couch. In a split second, he towered over Brad.

"Didn't I tell you to leave it alone?" Jerry said, his eyes lapsing into that fixed, stony stare that meant Golden Boy could now consider his butt kicked. "Didn't I tell you, huh, *boy*?"

Brad sprang up and faced Jerry. "Just be cool, Ito," Brad responded in his typical, lecturing fashion. "It's about time you started learning to live with other people."

Brad and Jerry stared each other down for a couple of seconds, the quarterback and defensive lineman reading each other's eyes. In a blur, Jerry's hands slammed into Brad's chest; Brad's fist found Jerry's nose, knocking his head back. Brad flew a few feet and landed on the floor, skidding on the britches of his Levi's.

Brad scrambled up, but before he could stand all the way, Jerry took two quick strides and knocked him down again. Brad's back smacked against the floor and Jerry jumped on top of his stomach, pinning him down, riding Brad and pummeling his torso with machine-gun fast punches. The hardwood floor underneath vibrated with each hollow thump. Bubbles of blood blew out of Jerry's nostrils.

Brad shrieked, "Stop it, Ito! Stop it!"

Davie Miles leaped out, catching Jerry's arm from behind, trying to pull Jerry off. Jerry's elbows flew backwards like he was grabbing a rebound, striking Davie in the chest and head. Davie stepped back, his forearms shielding his face. "C'mon, Jerry, cool it!"

Eddie and I double-taked each other. Was this the "little somethin'" Jerry promised us? Then how was I going to explain to my parents that I didn't do anything to keep my brother from getting killed by my friend?

We slid off the table and grabbed Jerry, pinning his arms to his sides as we tried to steer him away from Brad.

"Lemme get 'em," Jerry grunted to us. "Lemme go!"

Jerry twisted, turned, and took off at the same time, pushing us backwards with him into a run. Jerry's arms exploded up and out, breaking the hold; he sent me and Eddie and Eddie's hat flying, crashing into chairs. "What the . . . !" we both muttered in surprise as we peeled ourselves off the floor. We'd seen Jerry lose it before, but this was different. He'd never laid a hand in anger on me, Frank, or Eddie.

But Jerry didn't go after Brad again. We all heard heavy adult shoes breaking into a run down the hallway, turning into the SAC. Vice-Principal Buford showed up — impossible to miss at six foot six and dressed in his usual short-sleeve white shirt with wide paisley tie. Mr. Buford burst into the SAC and bellowed, "Ito! Get out of this school right now!"

"What?" Jerry yelled back, pointing to his bloody nose. "He did this to me! What about him? What're ya gonna do 'bout him?"

As Buford dropped down on a knee to check on

Brad, he shouted at Jerry louder than before, "I said get out!"

Jerry snatched up his coat and cassette player, then calmly departed as if he were used to it. Blood dripping from his nose left scarlet spots on his white T-shirt. Jerry didn't bother to stop the bleeding; he wanted everyone in the halls to see.

"Are you okay?" Mr. Buford asked, helping Brad up. My brother clutched his gut. "C'mon, let's take you to the nurse's office. Jeez! Never in my life have I seen two Oriental boys go at it like that. . . ."

As I righted some toppled chairs, I glanced over at Janet. She was watching me — with an *Are you okay?* look.

Why did she do that? What did it mean? She only stirred up my insides again, making me wonder why I always stepped on my brakes whenever I ended up anywhere near her. Would I ever find out? Sometime before she graduated? Would I even try to?

Sure, Dan! I wanted to yell at myself. *Go ahead and finally be good at something: avoiding what you want the most!*

I couldn't understand why I always did that. But when I found out, I hoped the reason why would be something tangible — solid, a thing in front of me, something I could tear apart like no one had ever seen. I would pounce on it with the force of a jack-in-the-box popping out on a shock-absorber coil instead of a flimsy spring. I would be like those little old ladies in the news — the ones who lifted the rear ends of trucks to rescue someone trapped underneath because they had no other choice. I would give physics classes a new problem to solve. I would . . .

I took a deep breath and jammed my hands into the pockets of my jeans. The reality was: I couldn't beat up something I couldn't see.

4. A four-letter word that had always intrigued me as a kid was "camp." And like the subject of sex, when adults acted as though I wasn't supposed to know about it, I wanted to know even more.

The way my parents and their friends used that word, it was about more than sleeping under the stars and slapping mosquitoes. When any *nisei,* Japanese Americans of my parents' generation, met for the first time, the first question asked was, "Which 'camp' were you in?" Sometimes my dad's buddies came over at night, bringing brown bottles of beer sweating in cardboard cartons with handles. As the men sat and talked in the living room, I overheard the word "camp" often.

When I was in eighth grade, I remembered asking my dad about "camp" for the first time. In the basement, he changed out of his grimy work clothes, after another day on the job as a Boeing machinist. "That was something that happened a long time ago," he replied without looking at me. "Today and tomorrow is all you need to worry about. We don't dwell on the past around here."

So, I had asked my mom. It was something bad, wasn't it? I prodded. As she chopped up more vegetables for dinner, she answered without looking up, "No use crying over spilled milk. *Shikataganai.*"

Huh? She-caught-what?

I later learned that this Japanese phrase meant something like, "That's the way it goes, and nobody can do a dang thing about it."

I had even approached Brad about the subject. He responded as if I'd ventured into forbidden territory, like I'd asked him if he had any dirty magazines.

"Yeah, the U.S. government did what it had to do, and we're good Americans and did what we were told. You think our government doesn't know what it's doing, stupid?"

Four years later, since my parents never said anything more and Brad hadn't added anything new, I figured I had to ask somebody else. Around the beginning of my junior year, I approached my U.S. history teacher after the rest of the class had left. Mr. Knox, the oldest teacher at Hoover and the social studies department head, made his students copy pages out of textbooks, grading us on how much we copied. Once, in the middle of the usual many pages of handwritten paragraphs, I added that the pioneers should've just beamed over to the frontier *Star Trek*–style instead of suffering through the covered-wagon bit. Mr. Knox never caught that; I still got my A.

He peered at me over the tops of his bifocals and grunted, "I don't care about any Japanese history. We only teach American history around here."

But these "camps" happened in the U.S. And people in the camps were American citizens. Didn't that make it American history?

"Look, son, I have a few months to cover over two hundred years. I only cover what's important."

Around the same time, the few Indian students in school, renaming themselves "Native Americans," started asking why their history wasn't taught. The "Chicanos" followed, wanting to know about Cesar Chavez and Wounded Knee. Together, we walked up to Knox's desk and asked for a class; Knox told us to get lost and accused me of being an "agitator." But when the Black Student Union got in the act, the administration created the class: comparative American cultures.

Frank didn't care for that class because he didn't think it would help his transcript for college; Eddie didn't think there would be any fine girls in it. Jerry said he wouldn't take any classes that weren't required to graduate.

And Brother Brad . . . he certainly had his take on me turning into an "agitator." One Saturday morning, as I sleepily awoke at the crack of noon, Brad confronted me in the hallway while our parents were gone. He raised his fist covered with a black glove.

"Is this the Black Power you love so much? You know why I got this on? 'Cause I'm not messing up my hand over you."

Boom! I felt those padded fingers square on my sternum, knocking me down.

"You don't make me or this family look bad. Understand?" he said as he stepped over me.

Thanks for sharing your opinion, Brad.

And it was only a matter of time before my parents heard through the grapevine that I was "causing trouble" at school. Dad showed up in the doorway of my room.

"You know," Dad said, "my parents had this saying: 'The nail that sticks up the highest gets hit the hardest.' You better worry about what other people will think."

● ● ●

I sat in comparative American cultures, watching Mr. Niles write on the blackboard. Niles was a first-year teacher, a young dude who never wore ties. He reminded me of Pete, the white-guy member of *The Mod Squad*. Niles worked up an outline of events that happened to Japanese Americans before World War II: Laws were passed so my grandparents from Japan couldn't become naturalized citizens. And they couldn't own land, couldn't marry outside their race, couldn't live anywhere they wanted to. Niles talked as he wrote, getting around to the war and wartime hysteria, leading up to the imprisonment of everyone of Japanese ancestry on the West Coast — including my parents' generation born in America.

The camps.

It was the first time I'd heard any of this.

Niles dropped his chalk in the blackboard tray, rubbed his hands on bell-bottom corduroy jeans, and pushed curly, springy hair off his forehead.

"So," Niles said, pointing to the blackboard, "even to this day there aren't any facts or evidence to solidly prove that those of Japanese ancestry in America were guilty of any acts of espionage or sabotage against the United States during World War Two. Therefore, the reasons why this happened must have been political and economic. Politicians did the popular thing to get elected; people wanted what other people had."

"But I think we were right in movin' 'em all out. They could've been a bunch of spies. How were we supposed to know? They bombed Pearl Harbor; what'd they expect?"

What the . . . ?

I whipped around in my seat. Greg Moore, who sat at the opposite side of the room near the windows, had spoken without raising his hand. He fingered the brim of his fedora on his desk; the hat matched his suit-length black leather coat and black everything else. Moore resembled Nat King Cole, dressed like James Brown, and talked H. Rap Brown — so what made him say something like that?

I pointed at the blackboard. "He just got done explaining they — we — were never proven guilty of anything!"

Only Moore's head turned with a minimum of movement. "But I think some of you were spies." He used his hat to point me out across the room. "We're at war now. With people who look like you. How do I know you're not a spy?"

A familiar feeling hit me, the same one I had when I was called a "Jap" or a "Nip" by other kids over the years, by guys into World War II movies; by adults on The Hill who formed those sounds under their breaths, or openly used those words since they didn't think there was anything wrong with them. My face flared up flaming hot, and my heart pounded quick and hard, pushing against my throat so I couldn't talk. I couldn't believe I was actually hearing this in *this* class!

"We're at war with North Vietnam," Niles reminded Greg, "not Japan."

Moore rolled on. "You and your people started it, man. You just got what was comin' to ya."

"*Me* . . . and my people?" I stammered. "I wasn't even born yet."

"Ain't you sorry you ever were?" Moore said. A few kids snickered with him, trying to be down. I turned to the other Asians in class. No one said anything.

Rhonda Du Bois, a junior who sat at the head of my row of desks, jumped in. "Are you listening to yourself, Greg?" Sitting a few seats behind her, I could see her profile — her short Afro, and eyes behind round wire-rims staring Greg down. "Calling him a spy is a really ignorant thing to say. Who's he supposed to be a spy for? The Sony Corporation? How long has that war been over?"

Moore retorted, "Whatever you say, Shirley Chisholm." Moore and his following snickered again. Rhonda Du Bois glared at Moore big-time.

Niles broke in. "All right! That's enough!" After all the chortling subsided, he calmly said, "You know what you're doing, Greg? You're playing right into The Man's hands. He wants the minorities to fight among themselves. Divide and conquer. . . ."

"There isn't goin' to be any Man pretty soon," Moore replied. "The revolution's comin', and I'll be there. . . ."

The bell rang; I glanced at Greg Moore, he stared back. *Right on,* brother. *I thought we were supposed to be on the same side. . . .*

Rhonda followed me out into the hallway. "Well, aren't you going to thank me for coming to your rescue in there?" she said behind me.

I just swung my head around. "Yeah . . . thanks," I muttered.

"Yeah . . . thanks," she said, imitating me. "I wouldn't have done that for just anybody. You owe me, Dan Inagaki."

Righteous Rhonda Du Bois about-faced and padded away in her usual white tennies and knee socks. My reaction to her then and there was the same as when she gave me the boutonniere during Homecoming: *What do you want me to do?*

Out in the hallway, all I looked at was the grimy linoleum floor, lit by patches of glaring white, courtesy of morning sunlight pouring in from the windows above the stairwells; those slanted shafts showed how much dust danced in the air. The seniors were lucky, I thought. In a few months their high school days would be mercifully squashed forever between the pictures and signatures in the Hoover annual.

I stared at the steps as I mindlessly ascended to the next floor. A bunch of bell-bottoms and flared slacks flopped by. High-heel shoes . . . legs in nylons, too? Then I remembered it was "Get Down Day" at Hoover, when we were supposed to wear some dressier clothes instead of our usual rags. I showed my school spirit by wearing what I wore any other day: my sneakers, my bell-bottom jeans, my half-button, half pullover collarless shirt that my mom said looked like a pajama top.

But then I checked out who was connected to those legs. I always seemed to run into a sophomore named Shari Jennings in the halls and just about every place at Hoover.

"Hi, Dan. How come you didn't get down today? I was looking forward to it."

I shrugged my shoulders. "Didn't care, I guess."

As she kept coming down the stairs, and I kept checking her out, her straight, chestnut hair parted in the middle fell around a mouth shaped into a *What are you looking at?* grin.

With her white dad and Japanese American mom, Shari was a rarity at Hoover and on Beacon Hill. And being different or unusual either worked for or against somebody. In Shari's case, her mix of races worked to her advantage, judging by the way guys looked at and talked about her.

Including myself.

More toward the start of the school year, Shari and her usual threesome of girlfriends showed up at meetings of the Student Senate, where I played junior politician as Student Senator for the junior class. After "agitating" for the comparative American cultures class, I found a note in my locker. "Right on! I totally support what you're doing." The note ended with "Luv, S. J." No girl had ever written me a note before. The first thing I thought was it must've been a mistake. I never said anything to Shari about it.

As she passed me on the steps, Shari, with her short dress wrinkling in its tightness, pulled my head around like a football face-mask penalty.

Anyway, what did Shari matter? Only attention from one person did.

As I worked my way up the next flight, Davie Miles descended the steps — with an arm around Janet Ishino's shoulders as he whispered into her ear. I tried to look the other way, but her eyes latched on to mine for a second, then pulled off and moved on — those eyes that must've made any guy feel like he was worth something. And right then, those eyes seemed to say to me: *What about you?*

I knew who would be in the library lying low, behind those oak double doors. Frank would be there after what had happened in SAC. Eddie would be there due to the ribbing he took for going ape in the locker room.

I spotted them at one of the long oak tables. Eddie was never hard to find since he stayed constantly in motion. If he wasn't jamming on his air sax, he was tapping on the table — Eddie the windup toy that never unwound. On the other hand, Frank could be hard to find: the bug that rolled into a ball upon contact.

Sure enough, Eddie had converted his Pee-Chee portfolio into a drummer's practice pad, using two pens as drumsticks. Frank rested his chin on his arms, crossed over a stack of unshelved library books. He gazed out through arched library windows at a painterly view of the Olympic Mountains, which reflected in duplicate off his glasses.

Eddie saw me and said, "Uh-oh, it's Eldridge Cleaver, and it looks like your soul ain't on ice, either. What's up, bro?"

I tossed my Pee-Chee onto their table and dropped into a chair. "What's happenin', most popular guys in school, yours truly included?"

Eddie rocked backwards with a laugh. "My, aren't we a little direct this morning. Man, what happened to you? You look like you're about to kill somebody."

"Not a bad idea, man," I forced out.

"Look out!" Frank said, chuckling.

"You guys know that Greg Moore?" I asked.

"You mean Mister Black Power?" Eddie said, holding up a clenched fist.

"Yeah," I said. "Well, in class, Niles was talking about us, about how there was never any proof that Japanese Americans were spies during the war. Then Moore says the camps were a good thing 'cause we're in cahoots with Japan — he said *I* could be a spy."

Frank lifted his head off the stacked books. "He said *that*?"

"Gimme a break," Eddie muttered.

"By that time, I was so pissed, I didn't know what to say," I continued. "It was like one of those nightmares — you know, the kind when you can't talk, when you have to yell or scream, but no sound will come out?"

Frank said, "You don't have to be dreaming to get like that."

Eddie cracked up and slid down in his chair. "Gimme five, man."

I cut in, "Did you know how bad our folks had it back then? Those camps didn't happen just because of Pearl Harbor. This country didn't like us way before then."

Eddie flicked both pens up into the air. "Man, you think our parents tell us anything about the past?"

"If they're even around . . . ," Frank mumbled. Eddie and I caught each other's eye, realizing we shouldn't discuss parents anymore. Frank pushed his chair back, stood up, and gathered his books.

"Where you goin'?" Eddie asked.

"Lunchroom," Frank said. "That's where the action's at."

Eddie said, "Yeah, well, don't be eatin' all that junk food and gettin' outta shape, 'cause we gots to play us some baseball." Eddie took a fake swing.

"Yeah . . . right . . . ," Frank grumbled, and walked away.

"Man, is he still bummed out about what happened in the SAC?" I asked.

"Maybe that, and looks like Frank can't qualify for a college scholarship he was countin' on," Eddie said.

"No kidding?" I knew how tight money was for the Ishimotos. Unlike the rest of our parents, Frank's dad didn't seem to care where Frank or his sister went to college, or if they even did. He didn't seem to care about anything ever since Frank's mom had walked out a few years before.

"Yeah, you know how it goes," Eddie said. "None of us Japanese folks are supposed to be poor enough to get some kind of financial help, even if we really are."

"Yeah," I added, "and we aren't supposed to rock the boat, either, by asking for a class on our history. Maybe that's why I'm not hearing about the chance to apply for any bucks."

"Yeah, ain't that the truth," Eddie said. He pushed his brim up his forehead. "You know, if you guys are still bummed out by what Janet said, I'd get over it. Man, she's just your brother's other half — tryin' real hard to be white. Seriously, forget her."

I wish it were that easy. . . .

Eddie looked past me. "Hey, Dan," he whispered, "that Shari Jennings? She's sittin' over there again. You know why, don't you?"

I shifted in my seat and saw her sitting at a table with her girlfriends, facing us, reading books. "Why?"

"Man, don't be naive, Inagaki. If I had your height, I'd be all over the place. Check it out, man, I'm gonna bring my next-door neighbor over here."

"Nah, man, it's cool. . . ."

54

"Hey, Shari," Eddie said across the tables louder than he should, "what's up, sister?"

"Hi, Eddie . . ." She ducked behind her book, since Eddie was starting to call attention to both of them. Her friends giggled.

"Hey, you better mow that back lawn of yours. It's lookin' pretty messed up."

"Oh, shut up, Eddie. . . ."

"Shhhhh!" The librarian ordered both to can it.

Eddie slouched in his chair, pulling his brim low over his face. "Man, check her out," he said. "Ain't that a good mix for ya? With her combination of genes, she's halfway there."

"Halfway to where?" I asked.

"To being the real deal."

"And what's the real deal?"

"What your brother Brad has, that punk!"

Eddie brushed his pen off the table. "Oops." He submerged beneath the table for a few seconds, then surfaced with a grin. The oldest trick in the book.

I cracked up, hands over my face. Eddie said a little loud, "Man, what'choo want me to be doin'? It's all look and no touch!"

Why did it have to be that way? I wondered what it was like to be a *guy* instead of the *guys we were.* I glanced over at Shari Jennings; she and her friends were laughing, laughing at us behind their books. I felt ready to explode into a thousand soggy pieces.

"Yeah . . ." I sighed. "As usual." I wanted to scream out the rest, but couldn't do that in school, let alone the library. *But I can't stand it anymore. . . .*

5. After baseball practice, Eddie, Frank, and I walked home from school by cutting through the nearby junior high playfield, massive enough to be divided into four baseball diamonds. Bits of gravel stuck into Eddie's leather heels, giving him some instant taps as he clacked along a cemented path running parallel to a Cyclone fence. On the other side of that fence, old men with potbellies straining the buttons of their cardigan sweaters teed off and putted on the golf course. The weather in Seattle was finally shifting to real spring, when the sun actually radiated heat and wasn't some elusive UFO in the sky.

And that meant Eddie would start heating up in his polyesters. "Hey, Eddie," I asked, "how come you always get so dressed up? Why the stylin' all the time?"

Eddie laughed his trademark cackle. "Gots to, man, gots to." He carried his usual faded black, steel-reinforced alto sax case that could've been glued to his hand.

"So, you get some practicing in on your sax today?"

"*Helllll* yeah!" Eddie responded, adjusting his brim. "*Every* day — you know that, Inagak. See, if I keep playin' and practicin' and get in a real tough band, I'll be ridin' home with some foxy ladies instead of walkin' home wit'choo guys."

That cracked all of us up. "That's cool," I said.

"Hey, you guys, wait up!" we heard behind us.

"Uh-oh," Frank said, turning around, "it's the cops checking up on me."

Kathy Ishimoto, Frank's older sister, caught up with us. A cheerleader at Hoover, she had on her cheer squad gear: red sweater, red pleated skirt, red kneesocks. If Frank was Charlie Brown, Kathy was Lucy, with the same squat build and jet-black hair, except Kathy's was absolutely straight and covered most of her back.

"Hey, Kathy," Eddie and I said. She was sort of an older sister to us, too.

"Hi, guys," she replied, books cradled in an arm. "So, how was baseball practice?"

"Same ol' thing," Eddie said, "you know, with

Dan's brother actin' all high and mighty — or maybe that's only when it comes to us."

"Ah, don't worry about him," Kathy said. "He's no better than you guys."

"Oh, yeah?" I laughed. "Try telling him that. . . ."

A voice sounded out from across the field. "Hey!"

We could see a figure in a white T-shirt and jeans sitting by a baseball backstop. Donny Hathaway's electric piano solo from "The Ghetto" blared out of a cassette player, getting louder as we approached.

"Hey, Jerry," Eddie said, "you get suspended again, man?"

"Yeah, yeah, just for a couple of days," Jerry answered, squinting in the sunlight. "No big fat hairy deal. School's almost over, ain't it?"

"Hey, I heard that!" Eddie and Frank said together.

"And Kathy's outta there for good," Jerry added. "Ain't she lucky."

"Yeah." Kathy sighed. "But, what after that? That's the scary part." I knew Kathy could've gone to any college she wanted. But she was going to stick around Seattle and attend community college — so Frank and their dad didn't have to be on their own.

Jerry pulled a rolled plastic bag and a pack of rolling papers out of his hip pocket. "Hey, Eddie, I got somethin' for ya. Remember our deal? You guys, too, you straight ol' Beacon Hill Boys."

Jerry let that bag unroll like a venetian blind and went to work: licking, pinching, rolling, licking.

"So, that's how you roll one, huh?" Eddie said. "I never rolled one myself."

"Well, now you know, moron," Jerry muttered through lips holding the joint. He lit it up and handed it to Eddie. "C'mon," Jerry said, "sit down and get your corny slacks dirty for once."

"You *guuuyyysss!*" Kathy complained. "You guys don't need to *do that*."

"What?" Jerry said. "And take everything straight?"

Eddie had never smoked before. None of us had, though Jerry had been on our cases to try. Frank, Kathy, and I stood there as Eddie squatted next to Jerry. Eddie sucked in and immediately exhaled.

"No, no, you rookie," Jerry said. "Hold it in longer."

Eddie took a drag and held his breath. When he could hold it no longer, smoke streamed out in a torrent.

"Whew!" Eddie said, falling backwards against the bleached green backstop with a thud, knocking his hat off. "That was a monster!"

Jerry cackled. "C'mon, Eddie, you just started. Hey,

Dan," Jerry said, offering the joint to me, "you wanna get high, man?"

"Yeah, man," Eddie said, pushing himself back up into a squat, "give those guys some."

"Nah, nah, it's okay," I said to Jerry.

"C'mon, Dan," Jerry insisted, "if you're worried 'bout Brad finding out and telling your folks, tell him I'll kick his butt again if he ever says anything."

It wasn't just about Brad and my folks, even though I knew my dad would make me the first Asian satellite in outer space if he found out. It was about family, community . . . belonging, as tough as that often was. Who wanted to be bad bacteria that the body has no choice but to expel?

And I could end up like Jerry, smoking the stuff and sitting in that field all alone.

"No, it's okay. . . ."

Kathy slipped me a half-smile.

Jerry held out the smoking joint to Frank. "Hey, Frank, *c'mon,* man."

"Don't you dare!" Kathy said as Frank stared at the joint. "We have enough to worry about. We don't need that on top of everything else."

"Well," Frank quipped, "you heard the boss."

Kathy shoved Frank's back. "Shut up."

"Well, then," Jerry said, rescinding his offer, "I guess me and Eddie gotta knock ourselves out."

"Man . . . this ain't nothin'," Eddie boasted, gulping in big chunks of smoke. He stayed stuck in his squat, staring straight ahead, his eyes a couple of wet marbles.

"Hey, Eddie," Jerry said, "so, how do you feel?"

"Do you guys feel the sun anymore?" Eddie asked, like it was so important. "I don't — it's just *there.*"

Eddie gazed at the sky and spotted a jet flying so high its vapor trail was string-thin. "Check that out. Needle and thread. Are they gonna sew some design in the sky? Maybe patch some rip in the clouds. . . ."

I cracked up with everyone else, but then I thought: *If that's how I'll look and sound if I smoke, I can do without it. I don't need any more help making myself look like a fool.*

Eddie mumbled as if he were talking in his sleep: "Hey, Jer, this is some strong stuff!" He eased himself up, leaning on the backstop for support. Jerry's tape continued with Donny Hathaway's rendition of "You've Got a Friend."

"Oh, *maaaaan,* Jer . . . I gotta go to work at my dad's store in a little while," Eddie said, his voice cracking with laughter and worry. "I'm messed up something fierce."

"Hey, it should be fun. It should pass by in no time."

"That's easy for you to say!" Eddie yelled back at Jerry, his voice now full of nerves. Frank, Kathy, and I surrounded Eddie as he started staggering across the field.

"You better believe it is," Jerry said, laughing.

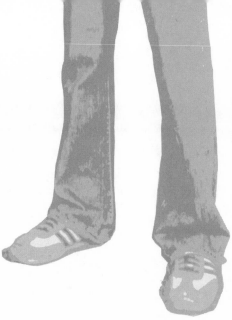

6. I sat in the principal's office, not because I was in trouble. Not yet, anyway.

Mr. Williams's office resembled the rest of the school: a claustrophobe's nightmare. He had nothing on the walls, indicating Hoover might not have been his dream job and he didn't plan to stay long. Rhonda Du Bois had insisted I come here with her, to the very top. And at the top was Principal Maynard Williams wearing one of his usual plaid suits.

"So," he said, rocking in his fancy fake-leather principal's chair, thumb and forefinger pressing his graying temple, "Mister Niles and his class isn't enough for you guys, huh? Now you want some books in the library to teach history from your point of view."

"Well, it's not my point of view," I said. "It's the other

side of the story that's never been told. Mister Niles is doing all he can, but what about outside of his class?"

Rhonda, sitting alongside me in one of the concrete-hard cherry-wood chairs, chipped in, "And that's how books in our library would help, so we can keep learning on our own. The Black Student Union totally supports this."

"This all seems kind of personal to you, Dan," Williams said. "And, believe me, I'm not against what you're asking for. But it seems to me, you also have a great resource within your own family. Have you asked your parents, asked them to tell their stories?"

I wasn't expecting the principal to be interested in whether my family talked about its past.

"It's like pulling teeth," I admitted.

"That's hard to understand."

"It is for me, too."

"Hmm . . ." Mr. Williams rocked in his seat a couple more times, then pronounced, "Okay, a few books aren't going to break our bank. If you provide the list, we'll see what we can do. But most likely, Dan, they won't arrive before the end of this school year."

Walking out of the principal's office and down the hall, Rhonda said to me, "See, Dan, we're a good team; we're doing some good around here, and we could have been doing this together a long time ago."

I didn't respond, heading to the SAC.

"I thought you had more ambition than that," she said. "You'd rather waste precious time playing up to social status that doesn't mean a thing?"

She was right. But I wouldn't admit it. "You have any better ideas right now?"

"Okay," she said, standing out in the hall, "you go and be a sheep, then."

But as soon as I stepped into the SAC, I should have turned around. Why did I always go there if I didn't want to see the show?

I took a seat on the red vinyl sofa, with Frank and Eddie. After taking a break for a couple of days, they had also drifted back to the SAC — human contact still beat being around books. Across the room from us, the cool crowd reigned, minus Banana Brad. At home, Brad never mentioned the fight with Jerry; he wasn't badly hurt, anyway — just a stomachache afterward. But the beating must've put a dent in his buffed and shined ego, and required a leave of absence from the SAC.

Instead, Jerry was acting like the conqueror, and he went about impressing the queen. He shadowed Janet, wearing bell-bottom jeans that day, and every once in a while slipped a hand around her waist. Janet didn't seem to mind, grinning at his comments, laughing at his moves.

"Ito's all over her, isn't he?" Frank said aloud, shocking me out of my trance. "You be a screw-off, use drugs, get in fights, get suspended . . . and score points with the finest girl in school, huh?"

Eddie and I were uncertain as to how we should react. Frank speaking his mind — especially about someone of the opposite sex — was not only out of left field, it was from somewhere out of the ballpark.

Eddie's forced giggle was too shrill. "Yeah, Ito wants some of that," he said, tugging at the brim of his hat.

I had to chip in. "Yeah, when they said the meek shall inherit the earth, it wasn't this planet they were talking about."

Humor must've been invented to ward off pain — if only for a few seconds. Eddie stuck out his palm, and we slapped five. Once again, Frank walked out of the SAC without a word.

We knew why Jerry had no problem playing up to Janet. If he didn't follow the Japanese American community's self-policing rules, he wouldn't be crippled by them, either. Jerry wasn't hamstrung by the voices in the rest of our heads, the "eyes always watching you," the "what will other people think?"

And why did Janet let Jerry do that to her? Somebody in her position — didn't she care what other people thought? Did she just enjoy the attention from the guys? Did she like the bad boys? Or was she putting on a demonstration for someone else? More than once, while escaping from the clutches of Jerry the octopus, those eyes pointed in my direction.

"Jerry!"

Jerry had just pulled Janet onto his lap.

"Hey, Jerry! What do you think you're doin'?" I spoke my mind and gave myself away.

"*Relaaax,* Inagaki," Jerry said without taking his eyes off Janet. "I'm just doin' what *you wish* you could. . . ."

"That's *cold,* Jer," Eddie said under his breath.

A few people tittered, and I thought I saw Janet trying to catch my eye. I couldn't look at her.

When I looked up, I noticed Kathy Ishimoto in another corner of the room, hanging out with a couple of cheerleaders. She was watching Janet and Jerry instead of following the conversation of her gang. I wondered how she liked the show.

From out of nowhere, Vice-Principal Buford filled the doorway — all six foot six of him.

"Ito, you know better than that," Buford said, his

voice commanding the room. "C'mon, you're gonna have to leave again."

Janet broke Jerry's hold and immediately jumped off of him. Jerry laughed as he said, "What did I do?"

"C'mon out," Buford repeated, jerking his thumb toward the hall.

Jerry stood up, and he wasn't playing anymore. "Yeah, but what did I do wrong?"

The way Jerry's eyes were lighting up, everybody in the SAC must've been asking themselves: Would he punch out the vice-principal?

"Are you threatening me, Ito? You want it to be for the day, or for the rest of the school year? Do you want to come back to this school, or not? It's your choice."

Jerry walked out of Hoover. Again.

I stood in the auditorium for an all-school assembly featuring a discussion about continuing or discontinuing U.S. military involvement in Vietnam. Some black students behind me ended the Pledge of Allegiance with ". . . and liberty and justice for *some*." Then a local radio news personality moderated a student panel, composed of members of Hoover's debate team.

Rhonda Du Bois ended her opening statement with, ". . . I agree with the stand taken by Muhammad Ali, that it is no business whatsoever of the black man to fight the white man's war."

The black students reacted right away. "Right on, sister! Right on!"

I faded out of the assembly, and my mind floated back to the same ol' place. In just a couple of months, I might never see Janet again; maybe that's what I needed — to not be reminded on a daily basis that there was still such a thing called impossible. But . . . why her? Maybe, after watching so many TV shows, after seeing the James Bond movies or flipping through the Sears catalog, I had concocted my vision of Miss Perfect. Add brains and her face — an Asian face — and Janet checked off on every category.

Forget about her, Inagaki! Suffering is what you're good at — no use snapping your streak.

The student-body president, a hippie-in-the-making who wore sandals rain or shine, talked about his friends' schemes to flunk the draft-board physical: "Some guys say they're going to walk into the exam holding hands, and then say, 'Guys really turn me on.' "

Waves of laughter rolled through the auditorium, with one piercing cackle lingering on and on — a crazed, assembly-stopping shriek that brought to mind The Riddler in *Batman*. Another round of the same solo laugh, followed by the student body laughing at the laughter, kept the panel from continuing. Mr. Buford did his Sasquatch-stomp down the aisle and yanked the perpetrator out. Everyone knew the giggler: sophomore George Mizutani, more commonly known as "Jive Boy."

With his googly eyes and parrot beak for a nose, Jive had wormed his way into the SAC's cool crowd by playing the fool. Getting high during school also helped augment his act, particularly when teachers demanded to know what Jive was doing sitting in classes he wasn't supposed to be in such as calculus and honors English. Jive wore black dress boots like Eddie's, with heels heard a mile away as they hit the floor. By the unevenness of the clickety-clacks, everyone knew Buford pulled — or dragged — Jive to the door. The auditorium's double doors burst open; a staccato burst of Jive's heels meant he was going down. And then there was a heavy thump.

As the audience went "Oooh!" I thought Buford had crossed the line — manhandling Jive, and suspending Jerry for the flimsiest of reasons. I would still go to bat for Jerry even after what he said to me. Like Jerry, Jive was almost an orphan, his family treating him like a runt in the litter. Jive was no athlete, no bright student, so, like Eddie, he had to become the entertainer, the joker, to survive among the Brads and

Brads-to-be. But none of those guys could keep up their acts forever. So, what did they do during their downtime?

Used drugs.

There had to be another way to feel good about ourselves.

Right after the final bell rang, I ended up in the principal's office again. And I didn't care if I was late for baseball practice.

I asked Mr. Williams how Mr. Buford could suspend George "Jive Boy," claiming he was high. He acts like that, laughs like that when he's normal, I said.

And how about Jerry? How could Buford suspend Jerry first, then come up with a "no hanky-panky" rule after the fact? That's what got him so mad — that a rule was made up just for him to violate.

Williams held up a hand. "Okay, okay, Dan. I'll have to agree with you that how Buford suspended these students may have lacked a little tact. Both George and Jerry were suspended just for today, and today's over. They'll be back here tomorrow."

Williams pushed back the hem on his suit coat and set his hands on his hips. "Tell me something, Dan. Why is it so important to stick up for these guys? You're not like them."

I said it before I even realized it. "Sometimes, you

feel like you have to do what you know nobody else is gonna do. . . ."

The next day, I was early for comparative American cultures. While I waited in the hall, another teacher walked out of the classroom.

"Hey, Dan Inagaki? I never really introduced myself. I'm Randy Reyes." He gave me the three-step, thumb, hand, finger-grip handshake. With his shoulder-length frizzy hair, round wire-rims, and black leather jacket, I had heard the rumor that some of the faculty didn't accept this hip Filipino teacher as one of their own.

"Oh, yeah," I said. "You teach math, right?"

"Right. This is my first year teaching. Say, I've heard what you've been doing around here, and Russ Niles just filled me in on a little more: that you advocated for the creation of his class, for books about us in the library, that you're standing up to Buford to stick up for our young brothers. What you're doing is really right on, and I want to rap with you some more about it sometime."

"Sure."

"Okay, catch you later, then." As Mr. Reyes stepped down the hall, he turned to me, holding a clenched fist. "Right on, man!"

This guy sure was down for a teacher.

That same day, I also ended up being one of the first to health class. I didn't know why I always got to class a few minutes early; I guess my parents' admonitions of punctuality had indoctrinated me thoroughly. Better to be early than late. As students trickled in, so did Janet Ishino, heading down my row of desks. "Hi, Dan."

"Hi."

Dressed in a white blouse with cuff links, navy blue vest with matching short dress, Janet didn't take her usual seat a few ahead of mine and a row over. She headed toward me, her books held to her chest, her high heels tapping on the hardwood floor with each even step.

My arteries swelled into garden hoses turned on full as she took the seat in front of mine, and turned to face me, the scent of her fruity perfume wafting around us.

"Dan, about what happened in the SAC yesterday . . . with Jerry?" she said quietly. "I owe you one."

She gave me that look I had seen before — the look that continued on, that still spoke after her words were finished. Then she turned to face the blackboard. What I would've given to know what she was really thinking. . . .

Out of the corner of my eye, I could see Frank watching us.

7.

I didn't get a break during spring break. My parents said their friend, Mr. Oshima, needed some help at his Baskin-Robbins right away. This was my chance, my folks went on, to land a job and set myself up for the summer.

I set myself up, all right.

Muzak played softly from speakers in the ceiling somewhere. A thin stream of water trickled into an aluminum basin used to keep ice-cream scoopers wet. Boss Man Oshima practically breathed down my neck as I stood behind the glass counter filled with cylindrical tubs of the 31 flavors.

"You have to be one hundred percent with the cash register, you know? You gave some of my money away yesterday. I came up short."

What *was* I doing here, wearing a white shirt, black slacks, and a paper hat with the word TRAINEE printed in bold across each side? How could I stoop *so low*? The boss continued with the requirements for working at his American Dream.

"I'll put you on the payroll next week after you work the night shift a few times and learn how to close up."

What?! More days without getting paid?!

But instead of saying that, I said, "I have to get back to school next week, and I'm still on the baseball team —"

"Of course," he interrupted. "You go to school, play baseball, and come to work afterward."

Mr. Oshima pushed back the paper hat on his head, exposing more crew-cut silver hairs as shiny as his square wire-rim glasses.

"So, Dan," he said, "if you plan to stick with it, you'll have to do this." Mr. Oshima passed an open palm over his head. Translation: Get a haircut. For his generation, that gesture meant a quick, close one from the *nisei* barber he and my dad went to — no questions asked.

"But, isn't it short enough now?" I pleaded, since I'd already had my hair cut above my ears before I'd started work there.

Boss Man shook his head. "You have to shape it up."

I'd sat in a barber's chair a couple of days before, watching my hair fall like black snow on that white sheet. By that time, it was too late *not* to listen to my parents.

I had to save what hair I had left. "What's wrong with half the ear showing, or something like that?"

"Holy smokes," Boss Man uttered, and shook his head again. "Why? All the guys you pal around with don't have their ears showing, or something? Heck," he grunted, "your parents are *nisei*, right? And they don't go for this longhair stuff, am I right? Huh, am I right?"

Yeah, yeah, you know my parents are nisei, *the kids of immigrants, second generation in America. You sound just like them.*

"You see Dick Johnson over there?"

I didn't see why Mr. Oshima always phrased his demands into questions, since he wasn't going to let me answer, anyway.

Dick Johnson, working behind another register, had his shiny blond hair tucked behind his ears.

"I told him to get a haircut, and now his parents come in here all the time and thank me and thank me for not letting their kid look like some gosh darn hippie."

The boss stepped closer and lowered his voice. "I'll be

frank with you, Dan. A lot of our customers are older folks, mostly *hakujin,* and they're not gonna buy anything from kids with this longhair stuff. They'll think their food has fleas in it or something, you know?"

Oh, yeah? I'll bet a lot of those older white folks are more open-minded than you!

Boss Man shifted out of his confiding tone and resumed the lecture so everyone could hear: "So, I'll expect to see your hair cut by tomorrow. And you better get with it and smile and be friendly to the customers."

Mr. Oshima left to inspect the rest of his all-American ice-cream joint, with scrubbed girls in ponytails and shorthaired boys behind the counter — especially the Japanese American kid who was even more American than the rest because he had the shortest hair.

Another week without pay. *Man, just because I'm your race doesn't mean I'm your kid, who'll work for you for nothin'.*

Another faceless customer stood before me, ready for some ice cream. I strained my hokey friendly smile, finding it harder and harder to do. *This is a joke.*

"Hi, can I help you?"

The weather showed me how I felt. Black clouds were scouring pads. The wind pushed around those passive, needle-shaped drizzle drops, some going up and sideways. Anybody who lived in Seattle long enough knew those drops wouldn't stay light and little for long.

I hoped Frank would get off work at the gas station and show up soon, before neighbors thought I was a burglar on his porch casing his house. Frank lived in one of the older wood houses on north Beacon Hill, a quiet neighborhood of similar homes sandwiched between two busy boulevards. Up close, I could see how the white house paint peeled and bubbled, uniformly covered with a thin layer of soot, when Frank's old Chevy rolled slowly down the street and pulled into a cracked concrete driveway. He stepped out of his car and said, "Hey, Danny, what happened to your hair?"

"Lost it for a job."

"Oh, yeah? Where you working at?"

"It's a long story. . . ."

"Well, it sure must be worth it."

"I don't know about that anymore."

Inside, I was greeted by the smell of dog and fry-cooking, a permanent fixture at Frank's place. I followed him down steep wooden stairs, to the coolness of his basement room. Frank flipped on the light, showing his sanctuary of stolen street signs, posters of state-of-the-art stereo gear, and his stereo components stacked on a shelf near the head of his bed. With his dog barking nonstop, Frank carried his oily gas-station coveralls into the garage. "C'mon, Sport, go outside."

Frank returned and fingered through a long row of albums on a shelf. He pulled one out and delicately set the shiny black platter on his turntable, then turned up The Stylistics' "You Are Everything." Falling backwards onto his bed and bouncing the springs, Frank asked, "Okay, so what happened, man?"

After I finished the long, sad story, Frank said, "So, what are you gonna do?"

"Not gettin' another haircut," I said. "What am I supposed to be? Bald?"

Frank said, "Nobody can make anybody work for nothing, even during a training period. That's illegal, you know."

"Oshima says everybody does it."

"Figures. Get free labor, any way you can. Especially from one of your own, 'cause they'll never do anything about it."

"Well, I'm gonna —"

"Seems like our own are our worst enemies sometimes, huh?" Frank said. "Reminds me of my mom and dad. They were so tough on each other, held grudges for stuff that happened ages ago, but easily shrugged it off anytime The Man screwed them over. Well . . . guess we're turning out the same way."

Yeah, but who says we have to?

As the falsetto lead singer of The Stylistics demonstrated how falsetto he could be, and as I went on about my soon-to-be previous employment — actually, volunteer work — I couldn't help but think back to last week in the SAC. The way Frank had stared at Janet, and what he had said about her before he walked out — why wasn't it obvious to me before?

"Sometimes, I think I could use one of Jerry's joints," I said.

Frank looked at me for a few seconds, then said, "I heard that."

We just sat there for a while, listening to The Stylistics tell us how "People Make the World Go Round." Then Frank asked, "So, did Eddie ever tell you how he made out after that time with Jerry on the field?"

"He said he never knew working at his dad's store could be so funny."

As Frank and I fell out laughing, somebody opened the door at the top of the steps. That door didn't just open — it flew open.

"Frank!" Kathy screamed, trying to cut through horns, drums, and laughter. "Frank!"

Frank shot up and turned the volume down. "What!"

"How come you haven't started dinner yet? Dad's gonna be home pretty soon, you know."

"I'm not hungry," Frank said more in revolt than as a statement of fact.

"What do you mean, *you're* not hungry?" Kathy yelled. "You're not the only one in this house who has to eat."

After a brief pause, Frank said almost to himself, "Man, Dad's probably not comin' home, anyway."

"Did you even go to the store like I asked you to?"

Frank looked like he wasn't going to answer, then mumbled, "No, not yet."

"Not yet!" Kathy shouted. "Well, I guess nobody eats tonight!"

The door slammed. The house shook. I heard stomping upstairs. "Jeez, what's goin' on with her?"

"Man, she's just tryin' to do too much," Frank replied as he turned the music back up, but not as high as before. "Keep up her grades, play mom around here . . . I don't see why she had to be a cheerleader. She needs to cheer herself on more than anybody else. What's she think she is, Super Sister or something?"

He high-jumped backwards, doing the Fosbury Flop onto his bed, his head smacking the pillow. He lifted his glasses off, setting the wire-rims on his stomach. The Stylistics crooned on and, before I knew it, Frank was asleep, snoring.

I felt bad for him. He and Kathy had it tough, while

I would just go home to a mom and dad who took care of everything, even if everything these days was about Brother Brad, the star on the field with a four-point-oh, bound for Stanford. . . .

I suppose I could have sneaked out through Frank's garage. But that seemed kind of tacky, so I gingerly stepped up the basement stairs, and passed right through the combat zone.

Still in her cheerleader outfit, Kathy glared out open venetian blinds in the living room. Frank was right: I always wondered how she could cheer everybody else on when she had to carry the load at home. But she wasn't so cheery now.

"Hey, Kathy," I said quietly and carefully, in hopes I wouldn't set off any kind of explosion.

Kathy turned around. "Oh, hi, Dan." She seemed to lighten up a little. "What's goin' on?"

"I gotta go now."

"What happened to Frank?"

"He fell asleep."

"Figures." She returned to the window; I guess we were done talking. Seconds ticked off into history as I stood there like a pole lamp in the living room. One thousand-one, one thousand-two . . . I made my move, and almost made it to the door.

"I never did care much for that Janet Ishino."

What the . . . ?

"Do you like her, Dan?"

I scrambled for an answer. "Uh . . . I don't have any reason to hate her, if that's what you mean."

What made Kathy ask that?

"She's lucky, looking like that . . . with everybody and everything coming her way."

Oh, man! I knew I should have left through the garage.

A halfhearted knocking on the door bailed me out. Kathy swung that solid piece of wood open, and there stood Jerry, with a feel-no-pain-and-won't-for-a-while grin. Eddie stood behind him with a similar, Jerry-made-me-do-it smile.

"Oh, hi, guys," Kathy said like she was expecting someone else.

"Hey, Kath," Eddie and Jerry answered.

"Hey, did we walk in on something?" Jerry said. "You can cut the tension in the air around here with a knife." Jerry made karate chop slices with his hands.

"Hey, Dan Man," Eddie said. "So, what'd you get a haircut like that for, anyways?"

"Was just talkin' to Frank downstairs. . . ."

Kathy clamped her hands on her hips. "Are you guys high again?"

"Why? Do we look it?" Jerry quipped. He and Eddie cracked up.

"You look like it, *and* you *smell* like it," Kathy said.

"Uh-oh," Jerry said, placing his hand over his mouth. "Secret's out, Eddie. So" — he turned to Kathy — "you want some?" Eddie couldn't stop laughing.

"No thanks," Kathy said. "We have enough problems around here."

Frank had just trudged upstairs. "Hey, what's happenin', Frank?" Eddie greeted.

"Not much," Frank mumbled as he flicked on the black-and-white TV with a screen the size of a cereal box and lay down on the living room's balding carpet. The TV faded in with a rerun of *Star Trek*.

" 'Not much' is exactly right!" Kathy growled.

Frank sprang up off the floor like a mousetrap set off. "What!" he yelled.

"How come you don't take care of what you're supposed to around here!" Kathy yelled back.

"I'm gonna do it!"

"When!"

"I said, I'll do it!"

"Hey, man," Eddie cut in, his attention on the TV, "this is the one when they have counterparts in a parallel universe."

"Yeah," Jerry said, "Mister Spock looks *bad* with that goatee, man."

"Yeah, I think I'll grow me one of them," Eddie added, stroking his jaw.

"Yeah, with what?" Jerry retorted. "The less than ten hairs on your chin?"

"Yeah, right. . . ."

Frank lay back down on the floor and stared at the television. After a couple of minutes, Kathy spoke up. "Dan and I were talking about Janet Ishino. . . ."

"Oh, yeah?" Eddie said. "What'choo say about her, huh, Inagak? I'll bet you wanna —"

Jerry's knuckles hit Eddie square in the chest. "Shut up, and let 'em talk. So, what have you got against her, Kath?"

"Just that she can get everything she wants, without lifting a finger," Kathy said. "So, Jerry, why did you get yourself suspended over her?"

Jerry said, "I just made a bet with Eddie here that she would go for a nice, innocent boy like me." Eddie and Jerry roared again, slapping five.

"And that was worth getting suspended over?" Kathy asked.

"Nothin' new for me," Jerry said after he quit laughing. "Besides, somebody has to do it."

Jerry never knew I went to the principal and stuck up for him. All that mattered to me was *I knew* I had done it. As Jerry and Eddie entertained themselves, I beamed back to that day before spring break, in health class, when Janet had thanked me for getting Jerry off of her. For me, her doing that was the same as getting the unexpected present I had given up on receiving a long time ago.

". . . Somebody needs to show Miss Everything Is Everything what a good time is —"

"Gaw, you guys!" Kathy said as she headed back toward the window. "Don't talk about her like *that.*"

"Well, you're the one who said you don't like her," Jerry said.

As Kathy peered through the blinds, something caught her attention. "Oh, my God . . ."

Kathy darted out of the house and out to the sidewalk. The new edge in her voice made me follow her out. All the while those guys had been carrying on, drizzle turned to rain, rain stopped, then rain fell and the sun shone at the same time. The setting sun finally broke through clouds, coloring the neighborhood coral. I followed Kathy's gaze to a block away, where someone with shopping bags was silhouetted against the sunset. When Kathy started to say something, the person turned away, heading down the block with short, choppy steps.

"Hey, c'mon back!" Kathy shouted. "It's okay!"

"Who is it?" I asked. Kathy didn't answer.

The figure stopped, glanced back once more, then shuffled out of sight.

8. I surprised my mom in the kitchen as she sponge-mopped the floor.

"I thought you were at work," she stopped and said, adjusting her glasses.

"I quit."

"When?" Mom's response wasn't as volcanic as I'd expected.

"I called him up a little while ago . . . said I wasn't coming in anymore."

"So, why did you do that? Don't tell me it's because of your hair. What's it matter if it's a little shorter?"

"It's more than that," I answered. "It's the fact that he won't pay me for almost two weeks of work."

Mom stroked a couple more wet strips on the floor,

then said, "He thought giving you a few quarts of ice cream to take home was going to make up for it."

Again, I was a little shocked Mom didn't knock me over the head with that mop when I told her I quit. She kept on cleaning, and I guess she was thinking while she worked. I couldn't recall her ever sitting still just to think — she would have considered that a waste of time.

"Remember Grandpa and Grandma's dry cleaning shop?" Mom asked.

"Yeah, sure."

"They spoke hardly any English, and most of their customers were *hakujin,* yet they still ran that shop for years. Grandpa worked that steam-pressing machine all day, and Grandma was always at the sewing machine. And in the mid-afternoon, when Grandpa needed some energy to get through the day, he ate a candy bar. Some days, though, he didn't have one. Maybe he couldn't take the time to go buy one, or maybe he couldn't afford one that day. So, you know what he did instead? He went to that sugar bowl, dipped the spoon in it, and *gulp.*"

Mom quit mopping for a second and made the motion of scooping and gulping.

"It was his own shop, so he could've gone in the back room and taken a nap. Or he could've even closed up for the day and gone home. But he never did. He did something like that so he'd have the energy to keep on working. That's all."

After a few more swishes of the mop, I finally said, "How come you never told me that story before?"

"Because I guess I never needed to . . . until now. I understand why you quit, but I thought you should hear that, too. Don't walk on the floor until it's dry, okay?"

Okay, I thought, hoping my dad's reaction to my quitting was even half as philosophical.

That night, the final Saturday night of spring break, I rang the doorbell and wiped my feet on the black rubber welcome mat that the Kanegaes had kept on their porch for as long as I could remember. The Ito family's Pontiac Tempest was parked on the blacktop road, where the lawn ended. Jerry was already here. I checked out the neatly cut grass. A cherry tree grew beneath the picture window; hedges had been trimmed perfectly flat on top. Through frosted glass surrounding the front door, I saw someone coming down the stairs.

"Hi, Danny," Mr. Kanegae said.

"Hi, Mr. K."

"Come on in. Eddie's in the shower, taking forever as usual. Hey, nice haircut. Now I just have to make

Eddie get one like that, too." Mr. Kanegae gave me a friendly wink.

I followed him up to the living room. "Have a seat. You've probably seen this guy before," he said, pointing to Jerry at the other end of the couch.

"Hey, Jerry."

"Hey, Danny," Jerry said, his greeting tame for Mr. Kanegae's sake. We both looked around the room, at the familiar collection of Japanese dolls in glass cases, and graduation and wedding photos of Eddie's brother and sisters. The TV was on in one corner, the volume turned all the way down.

Eddie's dad returned to his vinyl armchair across the room and pulled a handle on the side, popping out a footrest. Gray skies at dusk still cast enough light through the picture window behind Mr. Kanegae, brightening the flecks of silver hair that were quickly outnumbering his black ones. A small guy, he was really just an older version of Eddie. "So, Danny, how's working for Bill Oshima turning out?"

"I . . . uh . . . quit a couple of days ago."

Mr. Kanegae's face tightened. "What happened?"

"Well, for one thing, I worked without pay this week 'cause it was supposed to be my training week. And then he wanted me to do the same for most of next week."

"Are you kidding me?" Eddie's dad said, running a hand through his hair. "I think I might have to have a little talk with that guy. I wouldn't worry about it, Danny. A guy like you will easily find another job somewhere else. Yeah . . . no problem." Mr. Kanegae folded his arms across his chest. "Jerry and I were just talking about what he's going to do after high school. I told him, why not go to college like the rest of you kids?"

Jerry mumbled, "I don't think so. Blue collar is what I'll probably be the rest of my life."

"You're underestimating yourself, Jerry," Mr. Kanegae said, scratching one of his graying sideburns. "You're smarter than you think, you know."

Jerry smiled. "Hey, thanks. That's the first time I heard that." His face wore a pleased expression I'd never seen before.

Mr. Kanegae chuckled. "Long as you use your smarts for the right things, now."

"Of course." Jerry laughed.

We stayed quiet for a while. Mr. Kanegae was the only dad who even let Jerry into his house. Eddie's dad had known Jerry and me and Frank since we were little kids buying candy in his grocery store. I remembered Mr. Kanegae giving us packs of the flat bubble gum with baseball cards. Jerry's penchant to purchase without paying was notorious on The Hill, but he never shoplifted from Mr. Kanegae.

"So, how's your store doin'?" Jerry finally asked.

"Ah, it's okay," Mr. Kanegae replied. "In fact, we're doing well enough that we could hire some help. That's why I'm here at home now. Another guy is closing up tonight, along with my wife. Besides, the Missus and I could use a little time away from each other. Don't you think?"

Both Jerry and I shrugged and laughed, then we all fell silent again, watching the mute TV until Eddie's dad said, "This *All in the Family* is a pretty amazing show, huh? Don't we all know somebody like that Archie Bunker, regardless of his race?"

"I'll say," Jerry and I agreed.

Eddie called out from the basement, "Hey, you guys, come down here."

"Excuse me," Jerry said, standing up from the couch.

"Sure." Mr. Kanegae smiled.

I followed Jerry down. Eddie hot-combed his hair in front of the dresser mirror. Besides the dresser, the cramped basement room had a bed, two folding lawn chairs that Eddie threw his clothes over, and a stereo set with thigh-high speakers doubling as nightstands. Magazine centerfolds — Eddie's Greatest Hits — covered one sliding closet door. Whenever he was away, Eddie slid that door behind the other so his mom wouldn't see. He told her he needed to air out his clothes.

"What's happenin', pretty boy?" Jerry said, messing up Eddie's hair.

"Man, Jer," Eddie hissed, meticulously hot-combing it all over again. He snapped on a different comb attachment and said, "Were you talkin' to my old man?"

"Yeah, discussin' my future," Jerry said.

"Man, why you guys wanna get depressed?"

"What's that?" Jerry muttered, reaching over to mess up Eddie's hair again.

"Hey, we'll be here all night if you keep doin' that."

Jerry sat down and bounced the springs around on Eddie's bed; I leaned against the wall by the door. "Man, hurry up," Jerry said. "Why you tryin' to make your ugly self look any better?"

"What'choo talkin' about?" Eddie said. "Look, you never know who you might run into." Eddie checked his hair that looked full of body now, but would go limp in a half hour. "She's out there somewhere."

"In your dreams, that's where," Jerry said.

"Was my dad givin' you the third degree?" Eddie asked.

"Nah, we were just shootin' it," Jerry said, leafing through one of Eddie's magazines. "Your dad's all right."

"You just think that 'cause he ain't your dad."

Jerry tossed the magazine on the floor. "I'll trade you dads any day."

Yeah, Eddie's dad was all right. He knew how to talk to people. Except about one subject. I wondered if he would talk about the camps if I asked him. Or he might reply the same way my mom did: *shikataganai*. No use crying over spilled milk.

When we picked up Frank, Kathy wanted to go out, too.

"No way," Frank responded. "Guys' night out."

"Why?" Kathy persisted.

"Come *onnnnn.*" Jerry sighed, swinging his arm in an overhand pitch. "You guys keep arguin' all night, we ain't goin' nowhere."

Daylight still barely hung on as Isaac Hayes did his "Theme from *Shaft*" on Jerry's portable tape machine. Eddie sat up front, drumming on his knees. Jerry glanced in the rearview mirror at me, Frank and Kathy in the backseat.

"Look at all the squares together in back. Hey, Dan," he added as he braked for a red light. "You mean you got a haircut like that for a measly ol' job you didn't even get paid for? Man, you got taken for a *riiiiiide!*"

"No kidding," I had to admit.

"Jerry!" Kathy said. "Don't you think he feels bad enough about it without you rubbing it in?"

"Okay, okay," Jerry said. "You guys ready?"

"For what?" the rest of us responded in chorus.

"This." The light dropped to green. Jerry stomped on the gas pedal, tires screaming as we exploded forward — from the top of McClellan, the first street in Seattle to be closed when it snowed.

"Jerry!" Kathy yelled.

We hit the road where it leveled off — *whuumpp!* — then flew up in the air, all four wheels leaving the ground as we charged downhill again. The chassis crunched all the way down on the shocks when we hit more level pavement, took off, and then plunged down for more. Another level stretch of road, the oil pan scraped concrete, then we went up again and smacked down hard, knocking the exhaust pipe.

"*Oooh, maaaaan!*" I yelled as Jerry's Tempest flew one more time, landing on the street that flattened out at the bottom of the hill. Jerry jerked the steering wheel, screeching us into a drugstore parking lot, throwing us against one side of the car, then sped into a parking space and braked on a dime, pitching us forward.

"What's the matter?" Jerry said. "You guys look scared."

"Man, Ito, you wanna lose your license, or what?" Eddie said, putting his hat back on.

"What?" Jerry said, and grinned. "What's the matter with my driving?"

And who should Jerry park right next to? Alongside us was the familiar black Mustang: Brother Brad's car. Brad waxed that ride so much, it should have been too heavy to move.

Laughter erupted from inside the Mustang. Christine Holter, Brad's North End girlfriend, sat in the front seat. Davie Miles and Louie Chan yucked it up real good from the backseat. Louie and I used to be tight in junior high, when we were in the same class and he was just a regular sort of chunky kid. Then he discovered football and became one of the city's best, hardest-hitting safeties. He decided I wasn't popular enough to hang out with — even a liability — so he then did all he could to distance himself from me. He was in; I was out.

"Well, if it ain't the football team partying like they actually won a game," Jerry said loudly. As far as I knew, Jerry and Brad hadn't been this close together since their fight in the SAC.

Louie, with his cheeks flushed and eyes watery, poked his big head out the car window and said, "Hey, check out the haircut, man. Hey, Dan, did you just join the coast guard, or somethin'?"

"Coast guard . . . ," Davie and Brad snickered.

Davie rolled down one of Brad's windows. "What's happenin'?" he slurred as he spoke to me. "Hey, man, you gonna join the Black Panthers and carry on the revolution wit' the brothers? Gonna carry it on with your soul sister, Rhonda Du Bois?"

I thought of Davie with Janet. "What's goin' on, Davie?" I rebuked sharply. "Feeling all right?"

"Oh, yeah," he answered, grinning and oblivious to my tone of voice.

I heard Louie say in the car: "That's Dan's girlfriend — Rhonda Du Bois. Check that out." An eruption of laughter followed.

Jerry and Brad were trying not to acknowledge each other's existence. Brad leaned over and said something to Christine. She stepped out of Brad's car and headed to the store — with her long blond hair, tight bell-bottom jeans, and short black leather jacket.

"Whew!" Eddie said. "Is that girl fine, or what!"

"I don't get it," Kathy said, almost to just herself. "Why are they together?"

"You know any other Asian guy who can get something like that?" Frank sneered.

"*Her,*" Kathy lectured her brother. "She's not a *that.*"

"Well, whatever," Eddie said, "he's one lucky sucker."

I just wanted to get out of there. "Do we need anything from this store?"

"Nah, man," Eddie replied. "I think I just lost my appetite for anything."

"Hold on one second," Jerry said. He leaned over, shouting past Eddie in the front seat. "Hey, Brad! What's with the integrated car tonight? Having a little Neapolitan with slices of Banana Brad?"

With those fast hands, Brad pushed his car door open in a split second. Louie got out on the other side.

"Hey, hey, guys, come on," Davie said, trying to keep everybody calm. Davie motioned with his thumb for Jerry to take off.

"Hey, Davie," Jerry said, "I'll catch up with you later. You deserve better company than that." Jerry laughed and ripped a reverse out of the parking space. As he turned, I saw Brad out of his car, pointing at me — a warning not to do anything I wasn't supposed to.

"So, where are we going?" Kathy asked, once the car was back in traffic.

"We're off to see the Wizard," Jerry replied, handing his plastic bag to Eddie. "And this is the Yellow Brick Road."

"No thanks," Kathy said, answering for all three of us.

Jerry's tapes were always better than the radio, and his cassette machine played "Suavecito," by Malo.

"This Latin stuff is bad, man," Eddie said. "Check it out: The Chicanos got Santana and Malo, Native Americans got Redbone, the blacks have everybody, white folks have everybody else . . . who do we got?"

"Maybe we weren't meant for music," I replied.

"I don't need to hear that, Inagak," Eddie said.

"Sorry."

Frank chipped in, "Well, at least we got Bruce Lee — a star in somethin'."

"I know," I said, "but, whoopee, just one guy doin' something everyone expects of us, anyway."

Downtown Seattle rolled by. Endless lights and endless people, with couples on a weekend night strolling off to what could be.

Kathy turned to me. "Dan . . . what's going on with Rhonda Du Bois?"

Eddie, Frank, and Jerry hooted. Jerry cranked up Cold Blood jammin' to "Valdez in the Country."

"Okay, you guys . . . fine!" Kathy tried to say over their laughter. I owed them for getting me out of that one.

More of downtown zipped past as I gazed at the

couples dressed for a night out, envying the guys with long hair. I pictured myself in a cool black leather jacket on a downtown street with Janet, walking together out of one of those movie theaters or restaurants. . . .

Right. I couldn't even say a couple of sentences to Janet, let alone spend a whole evening with her.

Wait a minute. Was that her on that corner? Who was she with?

Go around the block again, Jerry! I have to see!

That's not her.

What was I seeing and thinking? Janet Ishino: Like in that Stylistics song, "You are everything."

Jerry hit the freeway, and in a monotone, Frank read all the freeway signs aloud as they appeared and whisked by. "One Forty-Fifth Street North, One Fifty . . . Jerry, where the hell are we?"

"Only one way to find out," Jerry said as he swerved down a winding ramp.

"Good job, Mister Sulu," Frank said.

"Aye, Captain," Jerry answered, imitating George Takei.

Glaring aqua freeway lights faded away, replaced by solitary amber spots breaking up long stretches of black. Wherever we were, it sure wasn't Beacon Hill.

Jerry drove on in the dark. Then we saw bright lights ahead, waiting for us: *C'mon, fellas, c'mon.* Zap! In a flash they enveloped us, on a four-lane boulevard with every square foot lit in blinding white. Now Frank had a bunch of signs to read aloud.

". . . 'Only you can prevent forest fires.' . . ."

Frank's monotone was interrupted by high-pitched squeals coming from a junky Thunderbird that had pulled up alongside us.

"Oiyo oiyo oiyo . . ."

What the . . . ?

The girls in the car pulled their eyes up into slants and made buckteeth.

Jerry glared at that car.

Uh-oh.

"Forget it, guys!" Jerry said slow and loud. "They're a bunch of dogs, anyway!"

"Ah, screw you, stupid Jap!"

As the Thunderbird sped past, Jerry hit the gas. The Thunderbird fed more fuel; Jerry did the same. Faster matched faster. Eddie scrambled for his seat belt.

"Let it go, Jerry!" Eddie and Frank yelled at nearly the same time. "Not around here, Jer!" Eddie continued. "Especially not around here!"

Jerry eased up on the gas, letting the Tempest glide to a slower speed. His fist slammed down at an angle on the dash top, rattling the whole car. "Damn!" he sputtered. "I can't stand that!"

"We know, Jerry. We know," Kathy said, leaning forward and rubbing his shoulders. "But it's just not worth it. . . ."

Nobody dared say anything more until Jerry had cooled all the way down. "How 'bout a little food trippin'," Kathy finally suggested, her tone soothing. "Aren't you guys starved by now?"

"Sounds good to me," Eddie said. "Whadda you think, Jer?"

"Yeah, all right. But I need to smoke a number first."

We all squinted, trying to adjust to the bright fluorescent lights as we stood in the line for the cashier.

"Why don't we let Dan order for us," Eddie said, his eyes bloodshot.

"Why me?" I asked.

"'Cause you'll be able to remember," Eddie answered. "Jer and me . . . uh . . . er . . . can't right now." Eddie turned to Jerry. "Tell Dan what you want, 'cause he's gonna order for us." Frank and Kathy shrugged their shoulders. The three of us managed to deliver the entire order to the brown-haired, uniform-clad cashier filling out the order slip. She ripped it off a tablet.

"Order up," a voice barked from the kitchen. The cashier set our slip on the aluminum shelf behind her, landing beneath all the others clipped to a rotating rack, as she lifted a plastic tray filled with burgers and fries.

We waited at the other end of the counter. Eddie played percussion to the restaurant shopping music, tapping a straw on the Formica as we watched everyone else in line carry away trays loaded with food we wished we had. Jerry started to nod off. Frank and Kathy stared into space. We were a long way from The Hill; I didn't even know where we were. Somewhere way, way north. It felt like it had been hours since we'd seen another non-white face, let alone an Asian one.

"Hey, Dan," Jerry eventually asked, "how long do you think we've been standing here?"

I checked my watch. "When did we get here? Around eleven?"

"Something like that," Frank said.

"Then we've been here for almost half an hour now."

"Maybe it's longer for us 'cause it's a big order," Frank said.

"Yeah, but not *this* long," Jerry said.

"I heard that," Eddie chipped in.

We looked up at the aluminum shelf bathed in scarlet heat-lamp light, now bare of any food on trays;

cooks stood around in the kitchen. Jerry pointed to the lone slip lying on the shelf. "I'll bet you that's ours. She did that on purpose."

"We don't know that for sure," Frank said. "Maybe she just forgot. . . ."

"Oh, get off it, Frank!" Jerry said, the edge returning to his voice. "All the orders were supposed to be on that rack. What's ours doing sittin' there?"

"Excuse me," I said to the clerk, "we ordered awhile ago. Do you know what happened to our stuff?"

She looked back, stepped over to the shelf, snatched up the slip. Glancing at it, she brought the back of a hand to her forehead. "Oh, I'm sorry. You know what? I set it down to pick up another order, and forgot to clip it to the rack. I'll get your order up now."

She clipped the slip to the metal circle and twirled it around. "Order." A cook slowly ambled forward.

Frank turned to us. "See, I told you that's what —"

Eddie pushed his brim up with a finger. "Well, ain't this a b —"

"You did that on purpose, didn't you!" Jerry yelled out. The rest of us jumped in surprise.

The cashier wheeled around. "Excuse me?"

"You heard me!"

The other customers, white teenagers and some middle-aged couples, stopped between bites and stared

106

at Jerry. The restaurant was quiet, save for the Muzak version of "Raindrops Keep Falling on My Head."

"Sir, I think you're going to have to leave," the cashier said diplomatically.

Jerry roared, "Wanted to make sure the Japs got theirs last, right?" He took a couple of quick strides around us, rapidly covering ground. The next word he shouted created a sonic boom. *"Right?"*

"Jerry!" Kathy tried to grab him, but she was too late.

"Right?" Jerry said, one more time. His fist pounded the counter, shaking the whole thing. The cashier flinched.

Her voice quavered, "You people need to leave. Now!"

With a quick sweep of his hand, Jerry pitched an aluminum straw dispenser off the counter. It crashed across the tile floor, scattering plastic straws. Jerry slammed his palms on the counter and started over the top; the cashier screamed and jumped back. Two burly cooks emerged out of the kitchen.

"Jerry!" Eddie yelled, his hat slipping off his head as he tried to restrain Jerry.

"Let go of me!" Jerry yelled. His tone was creepy, guttural. "Lemme go!"

Frank, Kathy, and I frantically grabbed Jerry's

shoulders and together we all tried pulling him toward the door. "C'mon, Jerry!" Eddie shouted. "Let's get outta here!"

"I ain't done!" Jerry screamed, pointing back at the cashier. "I ain't done with you, yet!"

We shoved Jerry out the swinging glass doors. Eddie headed back inside.

"Where you goin'?" I asked him.

Eddie looked back at me like I was crazy. "Gotta get my hat, man."

9. Brad's voice broke through my sleep — sounded like it came from the dining room. I checked my clock radio. What? Was it 5 P.M. or A.M.? I smelled turkey already cooked in the kitchen. When I woke up enough to recount chronologically, I remembered: I got up once during the day, and went back to sleep.

"... What's our Japanese middle names? I'm Toshiro. Dan's what? Kenji? And Steve's what? Ichiro? Maybe it would've been best if we didn't have anything to do with Japan anymore. Maybe we should've changed — or at least shortened — our last name."

"Yeah, maybe you're right," my dad said, sounding like he was agreeing just to be agreeing. "We should have names like you guys, huh, Chris: short and easy to pronounce."

I heard Dad and Mom, Brad and Christine, and even Steve guffaw as I made my entrance. My grandmother also sat at the table, her hands folded on her lap.

"Well, Dan has finally decided to join us," Dad said.

"Did Dan go to church this morning?" my aunt asked from the kitchen.

"Yeah, he worshiped in bed," my mom replied. "Dan was out late last night doing who-knows-what with his friends."

"*I* didn't do anything. . . ."

"Don't you have anything better to do than worry her?" Brad said, nodding toward Mom.

"Man, I already got one mother," I said, slipping into my chair. "Don't try and make it two."

"Dan!" Mom glared at me, cutting her eyes in Christine's direction.

"What about you and your friends drinkin' —"

Brad held up a fist, threatening to beat me to a pulp.

Easter dinner was starting out just great, folks.

My dad cut Grandma's turkey into smaller pieces. My mom sat next to him, wearing a flowered apron and constantly rising to refill the dishes. Younger brother Steve made a big show out of chewing his food.

"Dinner is delicious, Mrs. Inagaki," Christine said. My mother smiled at her plate.

"Yeah," Brad added, "you can't go wrong with traditional American stuff."

"How's baseball going, Dan?" my aunt asked. "Still warming the bench?"

Brad laughed. "And that's about all he'll ever do."

Steve cut in with some singsong jabber: "Dan's just a quit-ter."

Thanks. But my aunt wasn't through. "How's scooping ice cream going? How much are you getting paid? Minimum wage?"

"He quit already," Dad announced. "Can you believe it? Bill Oshima goes out of his way to give Dan a job, and he shows his gratitude by quitting."

"What'd you quit for?" Brad snapped.

"'Cause you're supposed to get paid for working, even when you're getting trained," I answered with increasing effort.

Brad responded, "Getting trained is just like going to school, and you don't get paid for going to school. You don't get paid for being an intern, either."

Dad jumped in: "That's right, huh? Heck, in our day, we helped our own out, pay or no pay."

Grandma mumbled something long in Japanese;

111

Dad ignored her and launched into his typical topic. "Hey, you know that Yamaguchi boy in Brad's class? Harry's boy? What's his first name, Brad?"

"Michael."

"Yeah, Michael. He's going to law school — one of those high-tone ones on the East Coast. Now there's a kid who's going to be somebody, I tell you. You know, Dan, if you applied yourself more, you could be doing the same thing. A doctor and lawyer in the same family — that would be doing pretty good."

Grandma spoke again.

"What's Grandma talkin' about?" I asked my dad, hoping to change the subject.

"Yeah, now what's she talkin' about?" Steve repeated.

"Something about kids taking care of their parents," my dad said, irritated that I had interrupted his success seminar. "She's been going on all day since we told her about the nursing home."

"Huh?" I said, surprised.

"Yeah, I know," Steve cut in, "talks all the time and nobody knows what she's talkin' about. . . ."

Mom said, "She's going to have to move into one."

I let my fork drop onto the plate. *Clang.* "You gotta be kidding."

"Afraid not," Dad said as he quit eating and folded his arms over his chest, looking down.

"What for?" I argued. "She can take care of herself. How long's she been living alone? And even if she needed help, she only lives, what — a couple of miles away?"

"Grandma was gonna eat her shoes," Steve said, giggling.

"Steve . . . just finish your dinner, okay?" my mom said. "We found her shoes in the refrigerator today. She's been doing stuff like that lately . . . getting kind of funny, you know?" Mom pointed to her own head. "And she could burn her house down if nobody watches her."

"She can live here, can't she?" I said. "Brad's leaving in the fall —"

"No way," Dad cut in. "With her mind going, this place will be a madhouse."

I said, "Yeah, but a nursing home? Don't you think that's cold? She won't be able to talk to anybody else there. She'll hate the food — who'll make her the food she likes? They won't even know what Japanese food is."

I glanced at my grandmother. With her head bent, she seemed resigned to not become a burden to anyone.

"She ain't gonna last in no nursing home," I blurted.

Brad changed gears on me. "You know, you may think talking like that is cool, and *your* friends may talk like that. But that kind of talk doesn't cut it outside of Beacon Hill."

Show off.

"Sorry," I shot back, "but I don't hang around the North End as much as you do."

Christine looked away, dabbing at her mouth with her napkin.

"Well, *you* going to watch Grandma all the time?" my dad said, his voice tense. "I guess maybe you can, since you have no job for the summer now. Old-age problems, Dan. And you're gonna have to wise up pretty soon, too. You're not always gonna be a kid, just messing around, quitting a job just because you don't like it, for crying out loud."

Everybody finished eating. Grandma stared at her lap, then spoke for a while in Japanese — soft and even like an engine on idle.

"Can't Grandma ever quit talking?" Steve complained.

"What's she saying?" I asked nobody in particular.

"Huh?" my dad grunted at being bothered. He listened, then said, "Jiminy Crickets! She's giving us a history lesson about the old days in Japan."

Brad retorted, "Tell her we're not in Japan!"

"About what?" I insisted to my dad.

My dad sighed and rattled off quick Japanese to his mother. Grandma went on for a while as Mom and my aunt began clearing off dishes; Steve ran off to watch TV.

"Well, what'd she say?" I asked.

Dad quit drumming his fingers on the table and dismissed what he had just heard with a swift backhanded wave. "She just said it was tough times back then. We've heard it all before. No big deal."

I had never heard it before.

Brad pushed back on his chair. "Well, we should get going. We're supposed to go to Chris's, too."

After all the "thanks" and "good-byes," my family regrouped around the table and carried on: about who they knew had what kind of job and how much money they were making and how successful they were with good houses and good cars.

I focused on Grandma, sitting there, looking a bit more content. Maybe talking about the past dislodged some good memories. Even though it was Easter, I thought Grandma was more like a Christmas tree. She provided the warmth, the comfort, the tradition. But after the magical day had come and gone, she would be thrown out to waste away in the backyard, strands of loose tinsel still clinging to her limbs in memory of the purpose she had once served.

Across the dining room table, Grandma looked up at me. Through her thick glasses, her eyes locked onto mine.

She seemed to know what I was thinking. The problem was, I didn't know what I could do for her.

The doorbell rang.

"Probably for Dan," Mom said.

"School night, you know," my dad said, staring at me as if to say, *After everything we talked about?*

Eddie, Jerry, Frank, and I sat in the Itos' Tempest. We rubbed fog off the windows with the sides of our fists, seeing in the streetlight beams how rain came down thick and fast. On residential Beacon Hill, any ground not paved or held fast by grass became a pool of mud: Instant Mess — just add water.

"Whose place we goin' to, anyway?" I asked from the backseat, trying to be heard over Tower of Power's "Back on the Streets Again."

"Davie's," Jerry answered as he drove.

"Oh . . ." He was just about the last person I wanted to see. And if that's where we were goin', weren't we headed to the wrong part of town?

We pulled up to one of those Beacon Hill split-level houses — just like Eddie's place. Just like my place.

"Davie live here?" I asked.

Jerry replied, "Where'd you think he lived at? In the projects?"

"No, I just thought —"

"We know what you thought, Dan," Jerry said.

Davie's mom answered the door, wearing a tailored teal coat and dress. I didn't expect her to look like Diahann Carroll.

"Hi, Mrs. Miles," Jerry said. "Davie in?"

"Hear that racket downstairs? That's him. Wipe your feet and come on in."

Jerry smiled. "Thanks."

Downstairs, in the dark, we headed toward Marvin Gaye singing "Inner City Blues." Behind the door of that basement room, we heard Davie joining in with the part about sending a boy off to die.

Jerry rapped loud on the door.

"Yeah?"

Jerry poked his head through. "What the . . . ?" Davie said. "Hey, Ito, what's happenin', man?"

Davie sat in near-darkness, lit only by a weak swamp-green glow from his stereo gear and candles flickering on a dresser. Another candle atop a dented metal trunk burned weakly in an ashtray, about to overflow with melted wax.

"Did we walk in on somethin'?" Jerry asked.

"Nah, nah, it's cool. Just a little holiday ritual. Hey, Can-guy. Frank here, too?" Davie said as Frank walked in. "And . . . Danny Inagaki? Man, if you brought some ladies, we coulda had us a party!"

"We thought they'd already be here with you," Jerry said.

"Yeah, yeah." Davie laughed. "Don't I wish. So, what's goin' on tonight, fellas?"

Jerry reached into his coat pocket and said, "Speaking of which —"

"Uh-huh," Davie said. "Speak of the devil himself."

We four visitors almost jumped a mile when the door opened and a hand came through, holding an angel food cake. "Here, offer your guests some of this," Davie's mother said. "C'mon, Davie, come and take it."

Davie set the cake on a stool and pushed the stool to the center of the room. "Well, you guys heard the orders. Knock it out. Easter leftovers. Guess I gotta get some plates and forks, huh?"

"Well, we might as well get hungry while we're at it," Jerry said. "Hey Davie, you think we could smoke in your room?"

"Yeah, it's cool," Davie said. "Hey, Frank, open up that window above you."

Davie, Jerry and Eddie sat on Davie's unmade bed. Frank and I sat on the metal trunk.

Davie held out the number toward me. "Nah, it's okay," I said, waving it off.

"Still got reputations to uphold? I can dig it," Davie said. "Not like us fellas over here, where it don't matter what anybody thinks of us, 'cause none of it's good, anyway."

After those three slapped five, Davie said, "Hey, Frank, how ya doin? Don't be like no quiet Asian, or Dan's gonna start preachin' to ya."

"Me?" I said as Davie and I cracked up. Then I stared at a framed photo on top of the antique dresser. Most of the burning candles stood around this picture, with its glass reflecting dancing flames when a breeze from outside wafted through. The young black army soldier stared back at me, the American flag behind him.

"Yup, Danny, that's my bro," Davie said. "Vietnam and all that mess."

I nodded.

"See, Danny, I know a lot of folks been givin' you a hard time 'bout you stickin' up for yourself and your people. One time, Greg Moore was braggin' 'bout how he put you down in class. And I jumped all over his mess, told him that if there were more folks like Danny "I" around, guys tryin' to get folks aware of what's really goin' on and what really happened in the past, then maybe my bro never would've gone to 'Nam in the first place.

"Yup . . . all the bros were the first to go. No student deferment for that kid. . . ."

The way Davie trailed off made the fate of his brother obvious. We all watched the floor and avoided looking at one another. After what Davie had just said about me, and as I thought about what I used to think of him, I didn't know what to say. "Yeah . . . sorry about that," I barely forced out.

"Nah, no need to be, Danny," Davie said. "That was back then a little ways."

"You know," Jerry broke in, "I make fun of these guys, callin' 'em college boys and stuff. But they're the ones gonna be gettin' that deferment. If my number's low in that lottery, and the war's still hot next year, my butt is gonna be in the rice paddies for sure."

"Drink a bottle of *shoyu* before the physical," Eddie said.

"A bottle of what?" Davie asked.

"Soy sauce," I said. "Drinking enough of that, with

all the salt in it, will send your blood pressure through the ceiling."

The bedroom door popped open, and we all jumped again as an apple pie appeared.

"Hey, Mom," Davie said, "I think we got enough now. We haven't even touched the cake yet."

"Well, why haven't you?" Davie's mom admonished.

" 'Cause we don't have any forks and stuff."

"Well, go get some," his mom ordered. "What's the matter with you? And why do you have your window open? Have you lost your natural mind? You're gonna make all your friends catch their death of a cold!"

The door snapped shut and we all snickered.

"Well, Davie," Jerry said, standing up, "we'll let you get back to what you were doing. Looks like you got a lot of dessert to polish off now."

"Yeah, I'll say." Davie laughed as he got up, arms raised while he stretched.

"So, do you feel mellow now, Davie?" Eddie asked.

"Yup," Davie said, "as mellow as you mellow yellow fellows. . . ." He stuck his arms straight out. "Just kidding!" he laughed. "Just kidding." Then he dropped his arms. "But really, fellas," Davie continued, "thanks for dropping by. It was cool."

10.

Misery didn't love only company, it loved a convention. So, the complainathon began during the first few minutes of being back in school after spring break.

"I need to learn how to make a scene, like Jerry did the other night," I said, describing my fantasy to Frank in the library. My haircut and the free labor still ate away at me, and I knew Frank would listen. "Jerry sure didn't hold back, and he wasn't even sure he was right. So, if I was gonna quit, anyway, I should've told Boss Man off while the place was packed with people. But, what did I do instead? I called him up later instead of saying anything to his face. And I didn't tell him off! 'Sorry for wasting your time,' I said. I apologized to him!"

"That's the trouble with us Japanese, man," Frank said as he altered his usual library position by lifting his head off a stack of books and sitting up. "Turn the other cheek and all that. Just suck it up and let somebody slap you around. Ever see your folks get burned and then just walk away? And then at dinner, all you're gonna hear about is what they should've done."

"I heard *that*."

Frank continued, "That was when my folks were still together. I remember, when I was a kid, my mother went up to the counter at some store. There was candy or somethin' I wanted behind the counter. She was there first, but the clerk kept passing her up to help the white folks. And she didn't say a thing. Not a damn thing. She just waited until the clerk finished serving everyone else. And, by that time, there wasn't any of whatever I wanted left."

Frank put his head back down, resting his chin on two clenched fists. "I'll never forget that. . . ."

"I guess our parents are still living like they had to during and after the war," I said. "We'll never know what it was really like for them back then, but they won't tell us, either. I know some people think they're a bunch of wimps for goin' to those camps. But if the country was screamin' for blood and a soldier came to the door with a loaded rifle and said 'move out,' or if

123

we were behind barbed wire with a machine gun pointing at us, I don't know if we'd all be so cocky."

"Yeah, learnin' history is fine and everything," Frank said, sighing and leaning back in his chair, "but that was then. What about us *now*?"

"Say, what?" I asked.

"Why don't we say what we want to right when we need to? How come you didn't tell your boss off like you wanted to? You were gonna quit, anyway."

My response was a reflex: "We just weren't brought up like that."

"Are we always gonna use our folks as an excuse?" Frank said, getting a little impatient with me. "What're you gonna do about gettin' paid for all that time you didn't?"

"Can't do anything. My folks told me not to even think about it. They said they're not gonna lose a long-time family friend over that."

"For real?" Frank said.

"For real."

"That figures," Frank snorted. "Fight among ourselves, tear one another apart, tear ourselves apart, rather than focusing that fight on whoever, whatever is against us. What's that saying? 'The nail that sticks up the highest gets hit the hardest'? Yeah, and it's our folks holding that hammer. And they'll tell us it's our own fault for getting whacked."

We both sighed, and then Frank said, "Maybe Jerry and Eddie are right. How can we take anything straight these days."

"Yeah," I agreed, tapping my pen on the library table. "I heard that."

Throughout my eleven years of public education, my great lunchtime fear was eating alone. But suddenly, it didn't matter anymore. I definitely wanted to avoid the SAC crowd and especially hoped Janet didn't see me, at least until she had to in health class.

I carried my tuna sandwich and carton of orange juice to the last table at the far end of the room and sat down. I stared at the cellophane wrapping on the sandwich, trying to block out the noise, the smell, the lime sherbert-colored walls of Hoover's windowless cafeteria.

It wasn't working. I wanted to leave, but walking away would have required the energy of running a mile. My clothes felt like they were made of lead.

I put an index finger to my head, my thumb cocked back.

Pooof!

If that were real, I could've taken out my own worst enemy. But with my luck, I'd land in a purgatory reserved just for me. I'd forever be the Asian guy in that Brylcreem commercial, trying to win a game that had already been decided.

A tray slapped down on the table, knocking me back to reality.

"Hey, Dan, what were ya doin', man? It can't be all that bad."

Eddie sat down across the table, along with Shari Jennings. "Hey, you know Shari, don't you?" Eddie asked, winking at me.

"Yeah . . . I see you around. . . ."

"Hi," she said, giving me one of her friendly, soft smiles.

"Meet my neighbor," Eddie said. "She's *always* askin' about you —"

"Oh, shut up, Eddie!" Shari socked him on the arm. Eddie laughed his high-pitched cackle.

"Your hair doesn't look bad," Shari said to me. "And quitting that job — that took guts."

"How much you been fillin' her in, Eddie?" I asked.

"She's the one that asked," Eddie said between mouthfuls of food.

"Appreciate it . . . ," I lamely replied to Shari, not

knowing what else to say. So, this was Shari Jennings up close, huh? She caught me staring, and went back to picking at her grilled cheese sandwich.

"Are you going to the meeting after school about organizing an Asian Student Union?" she asked without looking up.

"Yeah . . . how'd you know?"

"Mister Reyes is my math teacher. He said he shouldn't be announcing stuff like that in class, but he did, anyway."

I stopped sipping on my straw and asked, "Are you going?"

"Yeah, I want to see what's going on," she answered. "I guess I should have taken that comparative American cultures class, too. If you went to bat to start it, we should at least be in it, huh?"

I shrugged my shoulders.

Is that all you can do, Dan?

"You skippin' baseball to go to that meeting?" Eddie asked.

"Yeah. As long as Coach doesn't give me too bad of a grade, it won't hurt my GPA much." Who was I kidding? "Besides, he won't miss me."

Shari smiled. "How 'bout you, Eddie?" she said. "You going to check out this meeting, too?"

"Nah, I'm gonna jam with some guys in the band room after school. I'm gonna show 'em us Asians got the soul now and then."

"Okay," Shari said, gathering her books and lifting her tray. "So, I guess I'll see you later, Dan."

My eyes strayed down her top, then back to her face. Shari grinned — busting me. As we watched her walk away in her tight Levi's, Eddie delivered a back-handed slap on my arm.

"Hey, man, can't 'cha tell she's got the book on you? Lighten up and go with the flow, Inagak. You know what I'm sayin', man?"

When I got to health class, I kept the collar of my coat up, close around my neck, as if that would help cover my lack of hair. I sat in my usual seat in the back of the class, awaiting my sentence. Janet strolled in, dressed more casually than usual, in jeans and a T-shirt. She sat down in the seat in front of me.

"It's only hair . . . it'll grow back."

Her tone was sympathetic, which meant she had heard some version of my great spring vacation weeper.

She probably just felt sorry for me.

I had to face it: I wasn't in Janet Ishino's league. Being Asian worked for her — she called all the shots, I figured, especially with the opposite sex. Asian guys —

it was different. Even Golden Boy Brad had to prove himself. And if even he had to work that hard, the rest of us might as well call in sick every day. . . .

After school, I was back in the cafeteria slouched against a table. About twenty students were there — Asians who hadn't signed up for a clique in the SAC and had no other place to go. It figured that Janet or Brad didn't show — what did they need us for, anyway?

I watched water dry on the mopped floor as I listened to Mr. Reyes describe a guy he would bring in to teach martial arts, if that's what everybody wanted.

"I know you brothers and sisters have to defend yourselves from a lot of racists out there on the streets," Reyes said, standing with one foot resting on a stool, showing the zippered side of his black ankle boot.

Shari sat with her gang a couple tables away. I felt her checking me out and glanced at her; she snapped back to listening to Mr. Reyes. I wondered if she was really interested in our historical, social, political issues. She barely looked Asian. And since she was part Asian, she could identify with her other side and not be Asian anytime she wanted to.

"So, Dan, what ideas do you have?" Mr. Reyes asked. "You all know Dan Inagaki, right? This is the serious brother who got this whole movement started in the first place."

A few isolated "yeahs" and claps were heard. But most of the attendees at the first meeting of Hoover's Asian Student Union slouched farther down on their stools; some propped up their heads with their elbows; some stared even more blankly than they had before. Shari watched me expectantly.

I cleared my throat and said, "This is just the start. If you think it's been a long road to get this far at Hoover, then just think about everyone who struggled before us — our parents, grandparents —"

"Dan's right on," Mr. Reyes cut in. "There's a lot of elders, a lot of heavy brothers and sisters in the community that we can learn from —"

"Man, just sounds like more school," some guy in the group said.

"Okay, then what do you wanna do?" Mr. Reyes asked.

"You gotta get folks to join up, not scare 'em away," the same complainer continued. "Teachin' us martial arts sounds cool, but we do enough studyin' in school. We need to put on a dance or somethin', like the Black Student Union did last fall."

"Yeah, that's cool," a few mumbling voices agreed. Mr. Reyes scanned the rest of the group. Some shrugged their shoulders, some nodded their heads, others nodded their heads because their friends were nodding their heads.

"Any other suggestions, either for the rest of this school year, or for the summer, too?" Mr. Reyes asked. "Yeah, we should try to keep in touch year round."

For a few seconds, he got dead silence in reply. Mr. Reyes jerked his foot off the stool, sighed, and said, "Okay, we'll call another meeting pretty soon."

I knew Mr. Reyes was trying, but something told me this was our first and last meeting of the year. And from what I just saw, why not?

I got up in a hurry, trying to be the first out. I walked as fast as I could, my sneakers squeaking in the deserted school hallway.

Shari ran to catch up with me. "Hey, Dan," she said from somewhere behind me, "nobody says you can't do what you still want to do, what you've been doing all along. I'd be willing to help you out; you don't need them."

Still moving fast, I turned and said to her, "I sure ain't the only one who needs help around here!" I immediately regretted the gruff tone I'd used.

I banged open a heavy door to the parking lot and left Shari and that school in the dust.

11.   The last thing I needed to see was Brad's Mustang in the driveway. As I trudged up to the living room, I heard some rustling, but no voices. I had interrupted Brad and Christine, who both sat there on the couch like nothing had been going on. Brad's hair was still wet from just getting out of the gym showers. And Christine — *check it out!* — wore a skintight leotard top and jeans. No wonder Brad couldn't wait.

"You missed another practice," Brad said. "Your grade goes down every time you miss, you know."

"Yeah, I know." I was in no mood to hear that. But surprisingly, Brad didn't continue the lecture.

"Chris told me something you might be interested in," he said, gesturing to his girlfriend.

"I was just telling Brad something my dad told me

about my uncle in World War Two," Christine said, pushing strands of blond hair behind her ears. "He was a member of this Texas unit that got trapped in the mountains of France, just about two hundred left, surrounded, about to be wiped out. But then an all-Japanese American unit rescued them, with most of that unit killed and wounded doing it — a lot more than the two hundred they were saving. My dad called it 'the Rescue of the Lost Battalion.' And later, all those Japanese American guys were made honorary Texans. . . . I'm telling you something you probably know, aren't I?"

"I didn't know that," I answered.

"Was any of your family in this unit?" she asked, looking from me to Brad, who was picking at a hole forming in the knee of his jeans.

"Don't know," I said. "No one ever told us."

Chris furrowed her brows.

"Well, that's our history lesson for today, folks," Brad said, chuckling. "Dan's into that."

Brad threw me the keys to the family car. "You're taking Grandma to the cemetery — she wants to take more flowers."

"What?" I replied. "Didn't they just go there a few days ago."

"I know," Brad agreed, waving his finger around

his temple. "It's crazy. But if you like history so much, you'll like the cemetery, with all those dead people —"

"Oh, knock it off, Brad!" Chris said, her mood back to playful as she and Brad headed to the door. "I think he's a great guy to go out of his way for his grandmother like that."

"Dan-chan."

Grandma greeted me at her door. Her place always smelled like mothballs, so that meant she did, too. I caught a glimpse of the dark little living room of her tiny house, and realized I'd hardly been there in the last few years. She wore her usual dress hat with netting on it, and a wool coat, since the temperature of a cool spring day probably felt closer to freezing for her. Clutched in her arms was a bundle of Easter lilies wrapped in paper.

More Easter lilies?

My name was about all Grandma said that I could understand. I drove north on a highway while there was still daylight left, not knowing exactly where I was going but following a mental map of memories. A familiar supermarket, church, or turn in the road nudged me back ten or more years. Brad and I sat in the backseat of the family station wagon, jabbering constantly, with the car full of smells from all the wrapped flowers headed to the cemetery.

I spotted the iron fence with twisted black metal bars and sharp tips. A long time ago I'd thought of that fence as a whole collection of giant screws stuck in the ground. I turned off the boulevard and drove onto a narrow paved road, one of the many lanes winding through acres and acres of grass and headstones. A black Civil War cannon stood on a marble pedestal, marking the entrance to the veterans' section. Rows of small white crosses, hundreds across and hundreds deep, stretched along a hillside and continued over the top, seeming to go on forever. I slowly passed some mausoleums large enough to be small churches, complete with stained-glass windows. Carved into their stone were the same names as those on the giant department stores downtown. No wonder. And then there were the inconspicuous, square-foot square markers, buried in the ground and almost totally obscured by thick grass.

Where was that part of the cemetery where my family went to on holidays?

Grandma pointed me through a few more turns. Then the right names appeared on the headstones: Yamamoto, Sato, Suzuki, Fujii . . . nothing but Japanese names in this formerly segregated section of the cemetery. Segregated in life, segregated even in death.

I steered my folks' Impala toward the curb and killed the engine — thinking it was crazy to come here at this time of day, Grandma or no Grandma. A thick fog appeared ready to roll in, cutting off the last of the light. As I stepped out, my sneakers squished into soggy grass; water seeped through the seams.

"Damn," I whispered.

Flowers, mostly Easter lilies — some real, some plastic — stood in pots submerged into grass before the headstones. Grandma and I proceeded up one of the paths between graves, and I heard Brad's grade school voice.

"Don't walk over those humps in front of the stones. You're walking over dead people."

Now . . . where was it? Black gray, red brown, these slabs of marble all looked the same — it had been a long time since my last visit. A circle of white cherubs, holding aloft a marble bowl of spouting fountain water, marked the end of the Japanese section.

That figures. We don't know where we're going! But I should've realized that Grandma knew.

A rectangular, sepia-colored stone looked familiar from behind. And so did the columns of Japanese characters —a poem that I'd never asked anyone to translate. I circled around to read the name chiseled into marble: INAGAKI. A bundle of unbeaten lilies floated in an overflowing canister. I lifted the chilly can out of the grass and grasped the flowers Grandma had placed there before Easter. I poured some water out, slid the tin back into the ground, and dropped the flowers back in. Grandma went to work placing her new flowers in another tin.

As I shook water off my hands, I read the names on the Inagaki stone. Inscribed into an engraving of an open book was AKIRA, 1883–1955. The grandfather I never knew since he died the same year I was born. Next to his name was FUMIKO.

I glanced at Grandma, who was hunched over tending to her flowers. Why did they put her name on it already? I supposed we had to order in advance, get the place ready. *Yeah . . . we're so efficient.*

Below my grandfather's name was ICHIRO, 1925–1927. I remembered the yellowing pictures in the family photo albums, of the funeral for a two-year-old that never got to be my uncle because he tumbled down concrete steps.

"Are you both grieving for a loved one?"

What the . . . ?

I swung around and saw a chubby-cheeked woman with blond hair pulled back tightly into a bun, wearing a shapeless and fuzzy coat and clutching a pink rose in her hand. Fog had thickened and rolled closer, beginning to erase my car and the road. That woman, with her aquamarine eyes and flushed cheeks, appeared to have stepped out of one of those Ingmar Bergman movies on PBS — a Scandinavian mother comforting a lost child.

"No, not really," I answered when my voice came back to me. "It was a long time ago."

She nodded toward Grandma kneeling at the grave. "Your grandmother?"

"Yes."

"Is she Buddhist?" she asked, her sympathetic smile never wavering.

"No, she's Methodist, and my grandfather was —"

"Then you can be comforted in the fact that your grandfather is with the Lord now and will rest in peace forever." She stepped closer and, still holding her rose, grasped my hand with both of hers. A thorn was cutting into my skin. "Do you pray for him?"

A motorcycle sputtered through the cemetery road, its headlight beam piercing the mist. The cycle stopped on the road, and the rider yelled out, "We're closing up in fifteen minutes!"

"Okay!" I shouted back.

"Remember," she continued, moving my hand with

her gestures, "if you believe, then He believes in you, and all your loved ones and all the ones no longer with us will forever remain in His hands and never know pain or sorrow. Their life is eternal. Your grandparents were so exceptionally wise among your people, when they chose to finally find Him before it was too late, and they knew they were saved when they accepted Him."

That thorn dug deeper into my palm. "If you say so."

"I know so, and it makes my life so much easier. It can be the same for you. Please, pray for them every chance you get. And pray for those who still haven't accepted Him."

Her smile stretched wider than it had been.

"What would've happened to my grandparents in the hereafter, if they had been Buddhist?" I asked her.

Her smile unchanged, she squeezed my hand and let go, as if to say I should know the answer to that. Turning and walking away, her rubber galoshes left a matted path through soggy grass between the graves; she vanished into the fog.

A scary-movie chill dripped down my spine.

I glanced at my palm smeared with blood.

"Dan-chan."

Careful not to get any of that blood on her, I placed my hands underneath the armpits of her coat, helping Grandma up. As we headed back to the car, I wondered if all that had just transpired was real. To be a real Bergman movie, the whole scene would have been in black and white.

With vapor clouds marking her breath, Grandma smiled at me, stopped, and pulled a balled-up Kleenex from the sleeve of her coat. She gestured for me to hold out my hand. Grandma pressed on the cut, then wiped the blood off, leaving only the tiny incision. She stuck that tissue back into a sleeve and started walking again.

My folks wanted to put *her* away in a nursing home?

12.

Janet Ishino made her entrance into health class.

"Ooo-weeee!" a classmate hooted across the room.

Yeah, Janet couldn't be missed with that one-piecer she had on: The flowing flared slacks connected to the sleeveless top; the wide red lapels and off-centered brass catches stood out in sharp contrast to the rest in navy blue.

She took that desk in front of me and across from Frank — now where she always sat.

"Wow . . . what are you all dressed up for?" I asked.

"Student-of-the-Month pictures today," she answered, "as in the same pictures for the annual you guys will be in next year."

Frank and I chuckled. "Yeah, right."

"Hey, Frank," Janet asked, "how come Kathy's not going to a four-year college?"

Frank, with elbows resting on the desktop, said, "Doesn't think she could afford to do it now, I guess."

"That's a waste," Janet said.

"So, are you all set for UCLA?" I asked.

"Yeah, headed there in the fall."

Frank and I both glanced down for a second.

"How 'bout you guys?" Janet asked. "Where do you both plan on going? Both of you could get in some top colleges."

"Most likely University of Washington, just like everyone else," I said.

Frank added, "What else for any good Japanese kid? Going on to college is the same as moving on to the next grade in grade school — if you can pay for it —"

I cut in: "Except the smarter ones get to go to them out-of-state colleges."

"Yeah." Janet laughed. "And they get to pay a lot more for it, too. At least your brother got a scholarship to pay for some of it," she said to me. "Well, wherever you guys go, you'll do just fine."

The health teacher was late, so Janet asked Frank, "Kathy going to the prom?"

"Nah," Frank answered, "not into it."

I figured the real reason was because Kathy would

feel guilty about spending money on a prom dress when they needed the money at home.

"Sorry to hear that, too," Janet said.

"Are you going?" *Stupid question, Inagaki! Of course she is!*

"No . . ."

"Say, what?" me and Frank said.

". . . not that I know of."

"No way," I uttered.

"Why is it?" Janet argued, pushing hair back with her fingers. "You know what I am? I'm the one everybody *assumes* is going, so I never get asked. And I'm the one who's going to be sitting at home on that Saturday night —"

"Okay, people. Let's get going."

Janet was cut off by the teacher starting class.

I jumped into the backseat of the Ito family car. The interior now smelled like pine cleanser, courtesy of a deodorizer cut into the shape of an evergreen tree that dangled from the rearview mirror.

"You guys wanna hear some serious breaking news?" Jerry asked.

"What's that?" Eddie replied.

"Davie Miles asked Janet Ishino to the prom."

"Say, what?" Eddie said.

My heart didn't just sink. It fell over the cliff.

"Did she say yes?" Eddie asked.

"I don't think Davie got an answer yet," Jerry said as he drove. "If she went with him, she would have to sneak it, 'cause I don't think her old man will allow it. I know my old man wouldn't. How 'bout your dad, Dan?"

"No way," I answered, collapsing into the car seat. "Brad won't even bring Davie to our place."

"I don't think my dad would have a problem with that," Eddie said.

"That's why your dad is cool," Jerry said.

Eddie took off his hat and scratched his head. "I have some other earth-shattering news for you guys. Nixon ordered the mining of Haiphong Harbor. Russia and China are pretty pissed."

"Oh, *maaaaan* . . . ," I groaned, "World War Three's just around the corner."

"Yup," Jerry said. "Looks like that student deferment might be over for you boys. See you in Southeast Asia next year."

Nobody said anything more until we pulled up at Frank's place. Looking into the sun, I saw a familiar figure shuffling down the street, coming toward us.

"Hey," I said, "it's that same person who came around before."

Jerry used a hand to shield his eyes. "Looks like some lady with shoppin' bags."

The three of us stepped out onto the sidewalk and stared at her. As before, she dead-stopped. The same way a human stalker is trained to do when seen by an animal. And, as before, she pivoted around and slinked away.

"You think maybe we scared her off?" Eddie asked.

"Maybe she don't like us, whoever she is," Jerry answered. "But that wouldn't be anything new for us, now would it?"

Eddie and I snickered.

Kathy opened the door and let us in. "Oh, hi guys."

"Hey, Kath."

"Your brother in?" Jerry asked.

"Frank's downstairs with Jive Boy." Kathy seemed preoccupied.

"Jive Boy?" the three of us responded.

"Yeah," Kathy said, "he's been here lately. It's okay — he's good to us. He makes us laugh . . . besides, we know what it's like to need somebody to hang out with."

We headed downstairs into Frank's basement room. There, Jive Boy was in the middle of his jive rendition of Kool & the Gang's "Funky Man."

"I'm gonna funk everybody up. You hear me? Everybody!"

Jive Boy performed sitting down on a chair while Frank sat on his bed. As Jive's hands and feet waved around with the song, he looked like a marionette controlled by some spastic puppeteer. I realized suddenly that Jive's presence wasn't the only thing different about Frank's room. How come he endured Jive singing a cappella and not along with his . . .

"Hey, Frank!" I said. "What happened to your stereo gear?" Frank was missing an awful lot of hardware from his shelves.

"I got ripped off sometime today," Frank muttered.

"What!" Eddie cried.

"Somebody busted in the basement window. They took all the stereo stuff."

"Everything?" I asked like a dummy, when the answer appeared obvious.

"Yup," Frank nodded, "even all the cords. And they poisoned Sport to keep him quiet."

My eyebrows went up. "Poisoned? Dead?"

Frank nodded again.

"Man, that's cold!" Eddie said. "They did it today while nobody was home?"

"Yup."

"Did you call the police, and all that?" I asked.

"Yeah," Frank answered, "but what can they do?"

"Was all the stuff insured?"

"Are you kidding?"

Frank proceeded to divulge the bloody details; our imaginations filled in the blanks. Frank had strolled into his house after the baseball game. He tiredly thumped down the steps to his room, and when he landed on the concrete floor he could feel the disorder. Something was wrong. The entire basement seemed chillier. A faint breeze fanned through the rooms. The door leading to the garage stood ajar. Frank cautiously stepped into the garage. The door to the backyard was wide open.

A lower corner of that door's window had been shattered after it was covered with duct tape. A few shards lay scattered about the floor, some stuck to bits of tape. Frank put it all together: A fist punched through the taped window; a hand reached through and turned the dead bolt lock.

Everything gone: turntable, amplifier, speakers, headphones, over a hundred albums, reels, and cassettes, even all the patch cords. Three pencils lay gathered into a tripod, where the amplifier used to be. Take that, Frank Ishimoto! Ha, ha, we had all the time in the world!

Then Frank had spotted the furry gray body, huddled in a corner of the backyard against the basket-weave fence. He slowly squatted down and touched it.

Shreds of raw meat clung to teeth in a gaping mouth. . . .

None of us had budged an inch while Frank told the story.

"Don't worry, I'll find 'em," Jerry said as if he had already accomplished the mission. "I'll find out who did it . . . yeah . . . no prob."

We didn't know what to say or do next, but we had to conjure up something quick before Jive jumped into another song and dance. Eddie came up with the best he could do. "Wanna smoke a number, Frank?"

Frank and I gazed at each other for a few seconds, then both of us looked away at the same time. He needed it, and I understood.

"Okay, everybody outside," Jerry ordered.

To avoid Kathy, we filed out the basement back door, with its busted window. There was still some shattered glass on the concrete floor. We lined up on the side of the house facing the sun. Jerry got a number going and handed it to Jive Boy.

"Pass that to Frank," Jerry said. "He's first, man."

While Jerry drove me home, he made fun of me — I had to be home by a certain time to eat dinner. Jerry, Jive Boy, Eddie — and now Frank — planned to cruise and smoke some more before dropping Jive Boy off. I walked into my house, and the family was already in the middle of dinner. As I took my seat next to Steve and across from Brad, my mother sniffed the air.

"What's that smell?" she asked.

Steve snorted loud. "Dan stinks."

Brad cut me the iciest look ever and said, "Dan and his buddies are smoking now. And not cigarettes . . ."

My dad slammed his palms on the table, making the plates rattle. "See, Mom," he said, "I told you he was getting all potted up."

"No, I'm not!" I yelled.

"Hey!" Dad continued, pointing at me, "You either shape up or ship out around here. That's all there is to it."

"It's that group he hangs around with, Dad," Mom muttered. "That Ito boy . . ."

I pushed my chair away from the table. I felt heartbeats in my throat, just like when Greg Moore jumped all over me in comparative American cultures. This time, my voice had to force its way through. "I told you, I didn't do anything! Why can't Brad be the liar for once instead of me?"

Brad looked like he was ready to stab me with his fork. Mom wasn't being nicey-nice anymore when she stamped a foot on the carpet. "Watch your tone of voice, Dan!"

"How many times have I tried to tell him, Mom, but he just won't listen!" Dad said, shaking a finger at me. "You know why you ended up with a bunch of losers? Because *you* don't try to be good at anything. And why's that? Because you just quit! Don't get paid a few days? Instead of sticking it out to start seeing some money, what do you do? You give up and make us look bad in front of everybody! Who do you think you are calling Bradley names? You know why he is where he is? 'Cause he's got guts, he works hard. He doesn't give up like you. . . ."

I remembered another dressing-down like this when I was young, when my tears mixed with the milk in my cereal bowl. That memory and its current repeat caused rivers of tears and snot to run down my face, but I didn't care.

"Don't lecture *me* about guts!" I cried. "White folks burn you, and you just walk away. Well, I know where I learned to be a wimp. Like father, like son. And you guys goin' into those camps — a bunch of scared sheep."

Whap! My cheek stung. But my father hitting me for the first time in my life hurt more.

"You weren't there — what do you know! Huh, snot-nosed kid?" My dad stood over, me, his finger in my face. "What's the worst that happens to you nowadays? Get called some names? Heck, if any of us acted like that Ito boy back then, we would've been strung up a long time ago. *You* can work any kind of job — that is, if you wanted to. *You* can go to school, to college anywhere. We couldn't. We always had to work twice as hard as the next guy; our buddies died in the war to get *hakujin* to accept us. And here you go with your messing around, making us look bad. Sometimes you just got to shut up and take it like a man."

"WHAT DO YOU KNOW ABOUT BEING A MAN, ANYWAY?!" The words flew out of my mouth.

Dad's hand rose for another slap.

"Dad!" Mom shouted, freezing his hand in midair.

"Steve, go downstairs!" she ordered.

My little brother hightailed it out of there. Brad stared at the center of the kitchen table, as if he were too embarrassed to watch.

"Go on, you might as well hit me," I said, the room growing blurry again as tears poured down. "You might as well, I deserve it, 'cause I finally got the message: If you're not Brad, you're nothing, nobody. How are we supposed to feel, the ones who aren't, can't be and never will be? I'm just trying to find something to feel good about, to be proud of. I *want* to know what it was like back then. I'm not trying to make anyone look bad. . . ."

Brad pushed his chair back and stood up. I waited for his two cents, but he surprised me by walking out without a word.

Mom and Dad watched Brad leave. Past experience had taught me that if Brad didn't immediately rebuke what I said, his silence meant that I was either right or *could be*. He would never say I was. And with Eldest Son making his opinion known, Mom and Dad had to reexamine their stance.

Mom looked down at her lap, adjusted her glasses, then said, "We kind of gathered that the past was somehow important to you, Dan. But we just don't think so."

Dad rubbed his neck and added, "Yeah, we just do things the way we know how to do 'em, and the past doesn't matter much. Can't teach old dogs new tricks. You know . . . there are some things to tell you, but I just can't right now.

"Why not?" I sniffled.

"Well, when I can tell you, you'll know why." Dad shoved his hands into his pockets, staring at the floor. I knew both Mom and Dad were scrambling for more words to say, but it just wasn't their line of work.

"Hey, sorry I hit you," Dad said after awhile. "You okay? Let me see."

"Nah, nah, I'm okay," I said, pushing his hands away.

"Want to eat, Dan?" Dad said. "You might as well have your dinner. Come on."

"Nah . . . not right now . . . thanks."

Mom and Dad started clearing the table, bringing dirty plates to the sink, but leaving the serving dishes with food for me. I headed to my room. One Kleenex wasn't enough to help me breathe again.

13.

About an hour after the big blowup
with Dad, I walked out the front door and into the
mild spring night. No one asked me where I was going; my parents were talking quietly in the kitchen;
Steve and Brad were nowhere in sight.

I kept on walking . . . all the way to Frank's.

Kathy let me in without a word. If she knew about
what her brother had been up to earlier that evening,
she didn't let on. Instead, she turned to a sink full of
dishes and treated me like The Invisible Man.

Downstairs, Frank, Jerry, and Eddie were crashed
on the floor of Frank's strangely empty room. Without
any sounds, what else could they do?

"Hey, you guys," I said.

"Hey," Jerry mumbled, opening his eyes and slowly propping up on one elbow. He took me in, puffy eyes and all, and declared, "Man, you look like hell."

Frank sighed, smacked his lips, and kept on sleeping. Eddie lay still, his hat over his face.

"What's goin' on, Inagaki?" Jerry asked in a low voice.

I could only shake my head. "My old man," I managed to croak, "he just doesn't get it. . . . Ah, I just got it on with my folks, is all."

"Tell me about it," Jerry agreed. "I don't need to hear any details, 'cause I know exactly how it went." He stood up, stretched, practiced a swift punch through the air, and clapped me on the back. "I got something for ya, for all ya Beacon Hill Boys, that'll make you feel better — a lot better."

I looked Jerry in the eye and nodded.

"For real?" Jerry said, raising one eyebrow.

I think so.

"What I got, ain't none of us ever had before. I mean, this *will* blow you away."

Yes.

Jerry reached into the front pocket of his jeans and took out a small folded bundle of white paper. Inside was another piece of white paper, half the size of a stamp.

"I've heard this stuff can get you a little crazy," Jerry said as he cut the square into smaller pieces.

Good.

"It's called window pane," Jerry continued. "Acid. LSD. I've been wantin' to try this. But you, Inagaki — I don't know. I mean, you got everything goin' for you. And your dad — jeez, we're never gonna understand all their *nisei* ways, just like they're never gonna understand what it's like for us. . . ."

Oh, yeah? What do I have going for me?

"You sure, man?" Jerry asked, cupping a speck of white paper in his palm.

I don't know . . . how crazy is this going to be?

Yes.

Hell, yes.

Eddie sat with his feet dangling over the side of his brother's swimming pool, exhaling bursts of pungent smoke punctuated by perfectly formed smoke rings. His brother and the family were out of town. I vaguely remembered driving out to Mercer Island, and changing into his brother's too-big swim trunks. The Staple Singers' "I'll Take You There" blasted out of the stereo inside. I saw Eddie's smoke rings turn into white doughnuts that disintegrated, one by one, with a tinkling crash. The shards of frosted glass floated down to the surface of the blue water, an azure pane of glass with moving wrinkles. Headlights lit up all that lay beneath.

"Whole new world, isn't it?" Jerry's voice came from somewhere behind me, by Frank's.

"Pass that number on over, Eddie. Man, don't be bogartin' it."

Bare feet slapped on the warm concrete, and then, *whoosh!* Jerry was flying!

What're you doing, Jer! You're jumping into glass!

Next thing I knew, I was covered with water.

"Hey, Dan, you coming in, or what?"

"Hey, Jer, you just splashed out half the water in the pool," Eddie said. "Okay, look out." He scrambled over to the low diving board and took off, arms flailing. After hanging in the air for what felt like hours, he dropped straight down for a serious belly flop.

Splaaat!

Frank and Jerry's laughter bounced off the redwood fence surrounding the pool, and echoed among the trees. Off to my left, Frank split the water without a sound.

"Whoa," Jerry said, "check out that form." He climbed out of the pool and walked over to a cooler filled with cans of beer and food Eddie had raided from his brother's humongous fridge. I thought I could feel the ground move with each of his steps. I grabbed the edge of the pool to hold myself still.

Frank swam over. He'd always been good in the water, swimming with a grace he never had on land.

"Hey," he said, smoothing his hair back with both hands. "What's up? You okay?"

"Dan's trippin'!" Jerry's voice sounded so shrill, it felt like a drill boring through my brain. Before I knew it, his big hands pried my fingers from the edge of the pool. As I lost my balance, I had a flash of memory: me, standing at the edge of the deep end, during swimming lessons at the YMCA years before. Even as a kid, I couldn't accept the idea of leaving solid ground, of jumping into something that seemed to descend forever. And I remembered the lake at Boy Scout camp, the sun rays that cut through the surface of the water, golden ladders going down into the dark, with no end. . . .

A palm pressed between my shoulder blades, shoving me in.

I found myself wrapped in a cool cocoon, hearing only gurgles from the water I'd disturbed. My body unwound; I closed my eyes, thinking I'd finally found a place of total peace. . . .

Then I realized I had to breathe.

Just as my head broke through to the world, the sudden weight of Jerry's belly flop smacked me in the face, pushing me back under. I twirled along with the spiraling swirl of bubbles. Which way up? Which down? I looked for the surface. Why did it look darker than before? I kicked harder, my ears ringing as I ran out of air. My head bumped something solid. Did those guys cover the pool?

C'mon!

I pounded with my fist. Hard as concrete. I wondered what would happen when I couldn't hold my breath any longer. Wasn't water made of oxygen? Maybe I could get some if I just drank it in. How many times had I been so thirsty, I would've done anything for some water? Well, now I could have all I wanted.

Drink, Dan Inagaki, drink.

Bubbles carried my last breath away. Water rushed in, filling my emptiness. . . . Was this all there was to it? Was this all the life I would have?

The final time I opened my eyes, I saw fleshy forms approaching me from three directions, long black hair sweeping back as they cut through the blue. Why were they swimming upside down?

Check it out: Asian angels.

Water through the nose hurt like hell. The first thing I saw was Frank lifting his palms from my chest.

"Hey, Dan, you okay now, man?"

"What happened?" I managed to get out, between coughing spurts of water from my mouth and nose.

"Man, you tell us," Jerry said above me. "All we know is you hadn't come up for a long time, so we all dived in after you like James Bond in *Thunderball.*"

"Yeah," Eddie continued, "Frank got to you first, brought you up. So, what happened to you?"

I had to be able to breathe first before I could talk beyond two words. "Somebody jumped on top of me," I explained between gasps. "I couldn't break through to get air. I thought you guys had covered the pool or something. . . ."

"You mean, you thought the bottom was the top?" Jerry asked in disbelief.

"Man, Inagak . . . ," Eddie sighed.

"You're lucky," Frank said, putting his glasses back on. I took in the starless night, the slight breeze rustling the branches of evergreen trees, smelled recently cut grass, heard the music on the stereo. I was readjusting to being alive.

"Hey, but really, guys," Jerry continued, "nobody says a thing about this, right?"

"Yeah," Eddie and Frank agreed, "you got that right."

"Well, as we were saying," Eddie said, "it was Frank who rescued your butt."

Frank sat by me cross-legged. "Aren't you glad we were in Boy Scouts?" he said.

My heart was finally slowing from an all-out sprint to a winding-down jog. Every breath still stung, but I was breathing. I didn't think I'd seen my life flash before me. Still, I'd had a sense of disappointment, of having pages ripped out of my book before I'd understood the story or knew how it ended.

I might never have seen if my story had a happy ending.

14.

"How're your folks doing?" Eddie's dad had me cornered in his living room on a late Saturday afternoon.

A week had gone by, and I hadn't said anything to anyone about what happened at the pool. Baseball was over, and Eddie and Frank were working extra hours at their jobs after school. Jerry was AWOL.

"Oh, they're fine," I replied. The truth was, my whole family wasn't saying much to one another at home these days.

Mr. Kanegae stuck his hands in his pants pockets and jingled some change. I heard Eddie clomping up the basement stairs, after a day spent working at his dad's store.

"Hey, Dan," Mr. Kanegae began, "you ever notice

that your dad's Japanese is pretty good? Better than most *nisei?*"

"Yeah, he can understand and talk to my grandma in some pretty heavy Japanese sometimes."

"Well, there's a reason for that. . . ."

Eddie rolled his eyes and sunk down on the couch.

"You know your dad was in the army during the war, right?"

I nodded.

"You know what he did?"

"Are you kidding? He never tells me anything."

"Well, that's because he can't. He was M.I.S. — Military Intelligence Service. . . ." The way Mr. K. paused, it seemed like he was the gardener and I was the grass. He let that much seep in before he continued watering.

All right, Mr. K. — keep going.

"See, when we could join the army, or got drafted, men who were pretty fluent in Japanese got sent to a special training camp. Then they were sent individually into all areas of the Pacific. Served as interpreters, code breakers, translated Japanese messages, interrogated Japanese prisoners, persuaded enemy soldiers to give up. . . ."

Eddie made the "talk, talk, talk" motion with his hand.

"Some were at MacArthur's headquarters," Mr.

Kanegae carried on. "Out in the field, they had a *hakujin* GI as a bodyguard with them at all times so they wouldn't be mistaken for the enemy. The war in the Pacific couldn't have been won without us. MacArthur even said so himself."

I said, "So, if he was some big war hero, why didn't he ever tell anybody?"

Eddie grimaced and gave the slit-throat sign.

"Again, that's because he can't. We were forbidden, ordered, not to ever talk about this — classified. In fact, I'm not supposed to be talking to you about this right now."

"Why not?"

"It's still considered military intelligence, secret stuff that might have to be used again. I heard it might be declassified soon, but I wanted you to know so you can see another side of your father — the guy you think's always giving you a hard time."

I remembered Dad telling me there was something he might have wanted to tell me, but couldn't yet.

Mr. Kanegae smiled and said, "But, hey Dan, all this I just told you — you didn't hear it from me."

Eddie's dad and I laughed. I figured that, if I had him on a roll, I might as well work in another topic. "Can you tell me something about the camps?"

Mr. Kanegae laughed again. Eddie shook his head

behind his father. "Oh, no," Mr. Kanegae said, waving me off. "That'll take forever. Maybe some other time, Dan."

Figures. Why did I even bother to ask?

Mr. K. swiftly turned around and busted Eddie. "Isn't that right, son?"

Eddie, who was shaking his head, immediately started nodding it. "That's right."

Mr. Kanegae looked at his watch. "Well, I gotta get back to the store before the Missus gives me holy heck. What do you fellas have planned for tonight?"

"Nothin' much," Eddie said. "Just might go to Frank's, or somethin'."

"Okay . . . have fun."

When the latch on the front door finally clicked, Eddie said, "*Maaan*, I thought he'd never shut up."

Eddie and I were sitting with Frank and Kathy around the Ishimotos' tiny kitchen table, drinking pop and eating chips — dinnertime during that same sunny Saturday.

"What happened to Jerry?" Kathy asked. "Haven't seen him in a little while."

"Good question," Eddie answered. "Haven't seen him at school, either. But I think why he ain't here is 'cause he might be feeling a little guilty."

"About what?" Kathy asked.

"About what he did to Dan at my brother's pool," Eddie answered, eyeing Frank and me. "He . . . uh . . . uh . . . was being kinda rough with him, pushing him into the pool and stuff."

Frank and I grinned to ourselves.

A sturdy knock at the front door interrupted us. Kathy took a look. "Davie?"

Davie Miles? I didn't need to see him now.

"Hey, Kath. Jerry happen to be here?"

"Uh-uh," Kathy answered. "But you might as well come in. The other guys are here."

Davie removed his train engineer's cap and walked into the kitchen. "Fellas, what's goin' on?"

"Haven't seen him much at school, either," Eddie said.

"You don't know what happened?" Davie said. "Jerry kicked Jive Boy's butt behind the school building, messed him up real good after school this week, got some payback for ripping off my man Frank here. That's why he's lyin' *real* low."

"Jive Boy!" I said, shocked. I thought about when I fought against his suspension, about him acting like Frank and Kathy's friend so he could rip off one of his own because they were easy targets. Scumbag.

"Jive do it alone?" Frank asked.

166

"That punk?" Davie replied. "Are you kidding? He had help from guys at another school. Jerry ain't done yet."

Kathy brought a chair for Davie to sit by the table. So, this was the guy who might be taking Janet Ishino to the prom, huh?

"Hey, Davie," Eddie said, "you worried about getting drafted?"

"*Heeelll yeaaah!*" Davie said. "You heard the news. Looks like it's only gonna get worse. Louie Chan said his older brother, when he saw his low draft number in the newspaper, he ripped that sucker down the middle. Then he kept shredding it into New Year's confetti. My bro did the same thing. And that's about the last thing I saw him do, too."

We all went quiet, staring into our drinking glasses as we remembered the story about Davie's brother.

But then Davie said, "You got a bottle of that sho . . . what was it again?"

"*Shoyu,*" Eddie, Frank, and I said together.

"Yeah," Davie said, "you got any of that around here?"

As we all cracked up, I thought I heard the sound of weary feet climbing the porch stairs, followed by a weak knock on the door. "Somebody's here," I told Frank and Kathy.

Kathy peered through the peephole, then swung that heavy wooden door open.

"Mom, I didn't expect you!"

"Is your father home?" The voice was low and worn out.

"Uh . . . no. Come on in."

Eddie and I shot each other a look. We had seen those shopping bags with handles before. And we figured it out: She always turned away because we were here.

"I didn't know you had guests," Mrs. Ishimoto uttered, avoiding our eyes.

"It's okay, Mom," Kathy gently said. "You remember Dan Inagaki and Eddie Kanegae — they've been Frank's friends for a long time. And this is Davie Miles, our friend from school."

Davie stood up, while the rest of us didn't. Mrs. Ishimoto nodded swiftly in our direction. I barely recognized her. She looked almost as old as my grandmother. But when she passed Davie, her eyes drilled into him.

"We should get going," Eddie said, too loud.

"Yeah," I agreed.

"*I'm* the one who should get going," Davie said, about to walk out.

"No, you guys stay there," Frank said, part request, part order.

Mrs. Ishimoto let her crumpled shopping bags settle on the kitchen floor and then started loading produce into the refrigerator.

"Mom," Kathy said, "you don't have to do all this for us. I mean, it's not like we're starving, or anything."

"Never mind. I came all the way over with these, so I don't want to hear any complaints."

Eddie's knee jumped fast enough to keep up with sixteenth notes. Davie looked at us and shrugged, as if to say, *What's going on?*

Frank stood up. "Here, Mom, let me do it," he said.

Mrs. Ishimoto slapped Frank's hand away. Hard.

"Mom!" Kathy screamed.

Mrs. Ishimoto's pointing finger flew out at Frank. "Don't touch that food with your filthy hands! Filthy hands all the time because working at a gas station is all you'll ever do!"

"We're trying, Mom!" Kathy shrieked. "We really are!"

"Failures!" Mrs. Ishimoto shouted like an evangelist. "Failures, both of you! I'm glad I don't live here!"

All of a sudden, the spirit seemed to leave her. She spoke in a normal tone. "Frank . . . Kathy . . . I won't be coming back," she said without looking at either of her children as her gnarled hand reached for the doorknob.

"She says that every time she leaves," Frank whispered. He turned and headed downstairs to his room.

Eddie followed. Kathy turned to the groceries and continued putting them away methodically, crying as she did.

Davie approached Kathy. "Here, Kath, let me do that. Your mom isn't around to see whose hands are touching it now."

"No, it's okay," Kathy said as she knelt down. "It's okay," she repeated, slamming oranges into refrigerator bins. Then she collapsed with her hands on the dusty kitchen floor, crying and unable to do any more.

"Hey, Kath, come on," Davie said, lifting Kathy up. Kathy shoved her face into Davie's chest. "It's okay, all right," Davie said, hugging her. "It's gonna be all right, you'll see."

I watched Davie and Kathy. Davie's the one who took the initiative to do that, not me. I was a novice at giving comfort. I had never seen my dad hug my mom, as I'm sure Jerry and Eddie had never seen theirs do the same.

I found myself in a familiar situation: I could've said or done what I need to say or do when I needed to say or do it.

But someone else ended up doing it for me instead.

15.

I explored the back side of Hoover High, the place with the sweeping view of the valley below. I sat on some mossy stone steps, looking at the freeways under construction that ended abruptly in midair. Freeways to nowhere.

"Dan, where have you been lately?"

Did Shari Jennings always make that much of an effort to find me, or was she just a good mind reader? As she descended the steps and sat next to me, I wondered how to answer her question, if I could give her the entire picture. Accounting just for what had been happening recently would've been the same as showing up during the middle of a movie.

Could I tell her about Frank being ripped off, about how I'd had it out with my parents, about Frank's mom and what Eddie's dad had told me — the fact that we were *sansei,* our parents' children, and what an indecipherable enigma that was? Could I tell her about Jive Boy being the two-faced traitor after all I did for him? Could I tell her how I almost drowned because I thought a little white piece of paper would take me away from Beacon Hill?

I had a feeling that Shari was going to figure into my future somewhere, and I needed to spill my guts to somebody. She wanted to know, so I told her all of that. And as she sat close to me on the steps, elbows resting on her thighs, those big brown eyes locked onto mine the entire length of my confession.

"Okay, Dan," she said when I had finally finished. "What can *we* do about this?"

That Shari Jennings was all right. As a breeze lifted hair away from her face, I almost had the guts to kiss her.

"I know where we can start," I suggested.

Kathy, Frank, Shari, and I sat on seats up in the top concrete tier in the band room. Down below, Eddie and his alto sax were jamming with a tenor sax, trumpet, guitar, bass, drums, electric piano, and the beat of congas — blacks, whites, an Asian, and a Chicano all together. Students lined the wall and filled more of the band-room seats, heads bobbing up and down to the beat of "Can I Dedicate."

Eddie started up his solo, his face shadowed beneath his brim. When the chord changed, Eddie hit his higher register and he got the crowd going.

"Yeah!"

"Go ahead on, brother!"

Just then, Jerry muscled into the room. When he saw me in the crowd, he held up two fingers in the peace sign. I did the same.

Eddie peaked with a series of fast runs and then warmed down to the end. The crowd went nuts when he did. Eddie lowered his sax and stood there, his hands still on the keys, with a grin as wide as Puget Sound.

Frank, Kathy, and Shari joined in with everyone's applause. Jerry made his way over to us. "Did you know Eddie was that good?" I yelled over the clapping.

"Nah, man," Jerry said, shaking his head, "never knew he was *that* good."

We listened to the band play a couple more numbers, with Eddie blowing more hot solos throughout their set. After, while Eddie twisted apart his sax and packed the pieces into the case, we surrounded him.

"Hey, Eddie, give us five, man," I said, holding out my palm.

Frank asked, "So, you guys an official band now?"

"Yeah, looks that way," Eddie said, snapping his sax case shut.

"Cool!" Jerry said.

As I sat down to dinner, the setting sun shone strong through the kitchen window, coating the entire room with an amber glow.

"Bradley's got something to say to you," Dad said as we started eating.

Little brother Steve butted in. "You mean they're actually gonna *talk* to each other?"

"Shhhhh!" Mom commanded.

"Yeah," Brad began, "you know the Key Club at school?"

I rolled my eyes. "You mean you guys who wear those corny look-alike sports coats and ties and are a bunch of do-gooders at community events?"

Brad ignored my tone. "Yeah, they need guys to be ushers and help out on commencement night. I submitted your name."

"Well, thanks for asking," I replied.

"Come on, Dan," Dad interjected, "it's something you should do. You know, if you do all that activism stuff at school, but show another side of yourself by doing something like this, that'll help a lot."

Oh, so part of my sentence is to perform community service, huh?

"Yeah, but don't I have to miss a day of school to go to the rehearsal?" I asked Brad.

"Is that going to be any kind of problem for you?" Brad said. "You're smart enough to miss classes. If I didn't think you were, I wouldn't have submitted your name."

I definitely must've been dreaming.

After dinner, my dad poured sunflower seeds in a large turquoise ashtray he always used for that purpose. With the ashtray divided into two, one side was for the uncracked seeds, the other for the shells.

"Hey, Dan," my dad said, "come on out here."

I followed Dad out to a couple of lawn chairs on the back patio. The sun headed to bed behind the Olympic Mountains.

"So, what do you want to know about . . . about something in the past?"

My dad surprised me that he would just come out so willing. We hadn't had a heavy conversation since I'd asked him when I was a little kid, "What happens when you die?" But he just opened the door, so I was certainly walking in.

"You were in the war, in the army, right?"

"That's right."

"What did you do?"

My dad cracked a seed and ate the inside, the ashtray on his lap. "Well, I was there, did my time, but, sorry, no great war stories to tell you."

I grinned, for I already knew from Eddie's dad. I already knew I was looking at an unknown, unsung American hero.

"Okay, then," I said, shifting in the lawn chair. "How come you guys never talk about the camps?"

Dad just stared straight ahead, chewing on his seeds. "Well, I think for a few reasons. Maybe it's just too tough to talk about. And anybody who was there might have a different version of what was tough. What hurts you bad in the past . . . you bury it, try to forget about it.

"And speaking of burying, that's what we're good at. You know, *shikataganai*. It already happened, so pick up and move on. Like Mom says, 'No use crying over spilled milk.' That's a real Japanese way of thinking, and, of course, our parents were from there."

Dad tossed another couple of shell halves into the "used" side and went to work cracking open another seed.

"I don't know if anybody else thinks this way, but I think we never talk about it 'cause we don't want you kids to use it as a crutch so you feel like somebody always owes you for what happened to us, and start making excuses. I know we *nisei* tell you, 'You weren't there, what do you know?' But for you *sansei,* it's more a matter of 'You're here, so what are you going to do now?' "

I never considered family heritage — and pride in it — as a crutch.

"It may seem like we're so tough on you guys," he continued, "but that's why — we just want you to do your best with the way things *are.* We can't help it because our parents are *issei,* old-school Japanese. Sure, you can bet they were always on our tails, too, calling us *baka* — fool, idiot." Dad laughed with a seed in his mouth. "And, in a funny way, that was their way of telling us that they cared about us. Sure, they did, and they had high hopes for us. But, you know they would never say that. They just showed us by busting their behinds so we could have it better than them. Always looking toward the future, never the past."

I'd never heard my dad talk this much about anything.

"So, when you were doing all that rabble-rousing — uh, activism stuff — in your school, me and Mom were telling you to put a lid on it out of concern of what might happen to you in the future. Because, *we know* what happens to folks that stick out, who are looked at as different. Like I tell you, 'The nail that sticks up the highest gets hit the hardest.' Well, I do know this: I never would've had the guts to be one of those nails."

Now, Dad's ashtray was full of shucked shells. I had watched him the whole time and wondered: *Did he just tell me that he was proud of me?*

"Oh, by the way," Dad added. "Grandma's going to stay with us after all. Yeah, your mother and I talked it over, and since Brad is leaving in the fall, we'll try it. But you have to help us out, you know."

"Of course!"

With all I just heard, the sense of relief I felt ran a close second to that night at the pool, when Frank, Jerry, and Eddie robbed Death of one Daniel Kenji Inagaki.

My father and I hadn't realized that the sun had already set. Around our house, streetlights suspended from telephone poles ignited with a weak orange glow, then soon pulsated into full aqua brightness.

16. I still didn't see why I had to go to Brad's graduation rehearsal at the Seattle Center Opera House. Just to be an usher that night? As Brad drove that morning, anything I said was grousing about having to go.

"It'll be worth it," Brad assured me.

I didn't see how. I felt odd — I could count on one hand the times I'd ridden in Brad's Mustang. I also felt blasphemous for sitting in Christine Holter's usual seat.

I was given my instructions and then sat in the audience, watching the class of '72 rehearse amidst the plush red carpet and walnut-stained paneling of the Opera House walls. I watched Brad march up to the stage, practicing receiving his diploma. I saw Janet go up there, even dressed up for the dry run in a black chiffon dress.

Man. . . . Without her, how was every school day going to be the same?

And with the rehearsal over, I stood in the lobby, waiting for Brad.

"Hey, Dan?"

Janet greeting me in the form of a question was something different.

"Do you want to come with a group of us to have lunch?"

"Me?" When my voice caught up with my brain, I said, "Who's in the group?"

"Just a bunch of girls; don't worry, Brad's not part of this, if that's what you're wondering."

I saw Brad cross the lobby with his jock friends. He glanced my way, and I wasn't sure if he was grinning to himself.

With Janet? Of course! But some habits were hard to break. "You sure I'm supposed to go?"

Janet touched my arm. "Why else would I be asking you? I'll give you a ride home afterward. I owe you, remember?"

So, I finally got to ride in Janet's gold Capri, down to the Seattle waterfront, to a restaurant over a pier with ferries docking near by. Just as she had said, I was the only guy among the Girls' Club president, the student body v.p., one of the fellow HHEX officers, one of the cheerleaders . . . all races sitting there, acting like adults as Janet sat next to me. As far as what we talked about, to me the entire lunch resembled a typically disjointed dream in which I would remember only fragments of what happened. But there was one thing I wouldn't forget. Each person at the table had had some type of confrontation with Vice-Principal Buford's hormone-hunting morality code, usually with students being accused of wearing dresses too short. Janet praised me before the others as someone who had the guts to stand up to the school administration.

Then the ride home.

"Wow, you sure were trying to make me look good in front of everybody at lunch," I said to her.

"And you deserved every word of it," Janet replied, looking at me as she drove.

I still couldn't believe what I was hearing when she continued: "You know, I never told you this . . ."

Was this going to be what I'd always wanted to hear?

". . . but I've always had a lot of admiration for what you did at Hoover. Somebody in my position — I should've backed you up. That might have made your struggles more 'legitimate' — if you want to call it that. Doing the student exchange, there were times when guys came to Hoover, or I went to other schools, and they would leer at me, or treat me like the exotic foreigner, and I never said or did anything. I didn't know how to counter it. It's always been 'go-with-the-flow Ishino.' And I know your brother's like that, too. That's what we're good at, going with the flow."

I thought Janet never encountered adversity in her life — which went to show how much I didn't know about her.

"You've always been right, Dan. We need to stick up for ourselves. I never had the guts to do it, to pay the price for what I thought was right. Like you did."

Now that I had reached the highest mountaintop, I had to ask her. I knew the answer, but I wanted to hear it from her. "So, you didn't end up going to the prom?"

"No . . . there were too many issues there. Davie's a great guy and everything, but, of course, he would have to come over to my house and meet my parents."

Janet slowed for a light, and I tried not to stare at her leg rising to hit the brake pedal.

"Somebody else could have asked me, too."

She gazed at me, gave me *that* look.

Before I knew it, Janet drove up the Inagaki driveway.

"Thanks for the ride," I said, wishing we still had miles to go.

"Okay, Dan," she said, pushing her hair behind her shoulder. "I guess I'll see you tonight."

As I watched her back out, I wondered: After four

years of shooting looks across classrooms, lunchrooms, libraries; four years of spending Saturday nights listening to the stereo with her the subject of every song — was this finally going to be it?

I wore the Key Club's regulation square sports jacket with the corny coat of arms on the breast pocket. And complete with clip-on tie, I handed out the commencement programs at one of the doors leading to the Opera House auditorium. Frank passed through along with his dad to see Kathy graduate. So did Jerry and Eddie — that was one of the few times I saw Eddie without his hat.

As the school band started its plodding rendition of "Pomp and Circumstance," I was relieved of my ushering duties but had to wait as all the guys in their red mortarboards and gowns and the girls in white marched down the red-carpeted aisles to assigned seats in front. On either side of the aisles, from the seats, smiles flashed and flashbulbs popped. "Play ball!" some wise guys yelled after the last long note of "The Star-Spangled Banner" — just like they were warned not to do during morning rehearsal.

I found a seat next to Jerry and Eddie as Principal Williams spoke, followed by some school-board member. Too many other speakers followed, reciting poetry and hyping how rosy the future would be. Then came time for the diplomas, otherwise known as the Hoover High Popularity Poll.

As Brad's name was called out, he brought the house down as expected.

"Boo!" Jerry hissed, hands cupped around his mouth. Some parents turned around to glare at him. Eddie and I slid down in our seats. When Kathy's name was announced, Jerry, Eddie, and I whistled. And who should be right behind Kathy?

"Janet Marie Ishino."

I watched her break from the line and take the stage. As she stepped across the floorboards in her white high heels and white gown, a whopping applause erupted from the male side of the class. I joined in; Jerry just grinned. Eddie waved his hands forward and went, "Naaaaahhh!"

And after all the graduates were honored and the Popularity Poll rated every one of them, they sang the school song for the last time and tossed their mortarboards into the air.

Eddie turned to Jerry and me and said, "That's us next year. Can I get five on that, my brothers?"

Under crystal chandeliers in the lobby, Brad stood with my folks, along with Christine — in a white silk, flared-pants, low-cut jumpsuit! Brad shook hands with my dad, then younger brother Steve as he almost yanked Brad's arm out of its socket. He shook hands with my mom. As I looked around at other mothers hugging — squeezing the daylights out of their graduating kids — even Brad shaking hands with our mother was an extraordinary thing to be doing. Then he held Grandma's withered hand. Her eyes beamed through her thick glasses as she spoke a couple of sentences in Japanese.

"She said 'congratulations,'" Dad said. We all laughed together — the first time we had done that in a long time. And I had to contribute my bit.

"Well, congratulations, I guess," I said, shaking my older brother's hand. I couldn't remember ever having done that before.

"Yeah, thanks," Brad said with a clenched-teeth smile, which meant he had more to say. "You don't have to hang around us, you know." That smile relaxed into a for-real one.

Soon as I left my family, I ran into Jerry, Eddie, Frank, and Kathy. She just about flew into my arms.

"Congratulations, Kath," I said as I hugged her. "Where's your dad?"

"He's outside, waitin' for us," Frank answered.

Kathy was soon surrounded by classmates saying their farewells.

"Me and Jer are goin' outside for a little bit, too," Eddie said, winking at us. "You guys wanna come?"

"No . . . thanks," Frank and I said, shaking our heads.

The two of us stood in the lobby and watched all the handshakes and hugs and tears rolling down cheeks. And as we had seen so many times before, the crowd parted for *her*.

Janet approached us in her sleeveless white dress. Her hair lightly bounced about her shoulders with every deliberate step — as I had seen so many times in the school halls.

"Well, I had a great time being with you guys in health class," she said, holding out her hand to Frank. "Good luck, Frank."

"Thanks," Frank replied, his Adam's apple sliding up and down. "Good luck to you."

And then her eyes held mine. "Dan . . . best of luck with *everything* — next year and every year after that."

"Best of luck to you, too."

I let her hand go and watched her walk away — maybe forever. If there was such a thing as a broken heart, I just stomped all over mine made of glass.

Now, I was the one trying not to cry.

Frank and I continued to survey the carpeted room. Janet talked with now-former classmates, Brad and

Christine did the same as they worked the room. Kathy hugged Davie.

Frank turned to me and said, "Next year is gonna be *our* year. Right on?"

I firmly shook his hand.

"Right on."

17.

It felt strange back at school — not having Janet to look forward to, or Brad to avoid. During those last few days of the semester, students and teachers went through the motions, and so did I. Shari and I walked through emptier halls.

"How come you're so quiet today?" she asked. "Something happen last night?"

"No . . . it's just that things are different now."

"Okay," Shari said as she headed off to class. "I'll talk to you later."

As I proceeded down the hall, somebody was pulling up beside me.

"My, my, my, are we robbing the cradle now?"

Rhonda Du Bois would have to show up. And what she said made me react as if somebody had opened up and read my mail. "Honing your spying skills, are you?" I said. "Practicing for a career with the CIA?"

"Nobody needs to waste precious time spying on you when you have it slapped on a billboard."

"She's a colleague," I retorted. "Okay?"

"Colleague!" Rhonda laughed a wicked one. "A colleague in what? Well, that's just too bad, 'cause the one who really likes you is gonna be heartbroken now."

"What . . . who're you talkin' about?"

"That's for you to find out, and maybe you'll learn a valuable lesson along the way."

"C'mon, you might as well tell me." There was only one person I wished she would name.

Rhonda held her ground. "Well, actually I can think of a couple. But I'll tell you this: The one who really adores you, you won't even give the time of day."

"You sure know how to make my life miserable, Rhonda Du Bois."

"Because I know you better than you know yourself, Dan Inagaki."

Then she swerved right in front of me, making me stop.

"But now on to some equally serious matters," she said face-to-face. "How's your Asian Student Union? I hear it isn't faring too well."

"Mine? And you're right — it doesn't really exist."

"It's going to take time," Rhonda said, her tone of voice changing. "The Black Student Union didn't happen overnight. And it's going to take a *leader*. So, you know what? B.S.U. is having its final meeting of the year tomorrow morning, before school. We'll be discussing activities and goals for next year. Of course, without any seniors here anymore, the new officers will be in charge. So, come and check us out . . . you're looking at next year's president."

I took a moment to let that sink in. Then she said, "We're going to shake things up around here next year. Both of us. Right on?"

I sighed for a second, then grasped her raised hand. "Right on."

Before leaving me, she said, "Oh, and you can bring your *colleague* with you, if you like."

But even my little skirmish with Rhonda didn't change how I felt. At lunch, Jerry and Eddie noticed.

"What's the matter wit'choo today, Inagaki?" Eddie asked. Frank cut me a look.

"Nah, nothin' . . ."

"C'mon, Danny," Jerry interjected, "it ain't . . ."

". . . the end of the world," Eddie added.

Real friends could do that kind of thing — read each other's minds and finish each other's sentences.

And, as I sat in health class with Frank, staring at

that empty desk in front of me, was when I really knew the size of that hollowness inside.

"Your heart's hurtin' 'cause you really miss her, don't you?" Frank said, pushing up his glasses.

I avoided looking at him, and nodded.

I couldn't rid myself of the emptiness after school, during dinner, before night fell.

"I'm gonna use the car — just going to Frank's for a little while, okay?"

I drove down Beacon Avenue, made the turn. I rounded the corner to another familiar street, to an address I had looked up in the phone book long ago, to the place I had rode past often on my bike, to the residence with the phone number I'd called many times only to hang up.

The porch light was on at Janet Ishino's house. A moth fluttered around the glow. I drove to the other side of the street and parked by a dark, wooded area. Inside the house, closed living room curtains reflected dull lamplight.

I relived the many times I had rehearsed an evening out with Janet. Before I had my driver's license, I would sit behind the wheel of our Impala. In reality, the car never left the driveway, and my parents, if they saw me, must've thought I'd lost my mind. The only thing that had changed since then was that I could ac-

tually drive, but the subject of my imagination remained the same. But, then and there in front of
Janet's place, I let myself play it out one last time. . . .

*Only his newest and best clothes will do on a night
like this, because was there ever one like it? When that
all-he-could-ever-think-about night arrives, he has no
problem finding her house because he has rehearsed
the trip so many times, and scales those concrete steps,
pushes the doorbell button. He still can't believe it —
that he is finally here and only for her.*

"I'll get it. . . ."

*Was that her? He can hear the padding of footsteps
on carpet as he begins to get the same rush as he did
when every day drew closer to Christmas. The doorknob clicks and turns, the door slowly draws open.
There she is, and it is impossible to single out every de-
tail: the earrings, necklace, shoes, fragrance of her perfume, the cut and color of her dress. She always looks
good, but never like this.*

*She introduces him to her father, who gets off the
couch in front of the TV to shake hands. He says
something as witty as possible, her father laughs, and
with the let's-get-it-over-with list of pleasantries ex-
hausted, she says, "Well, shall we go?"*

"Nice meeting you."

"Okay. You kids have fun."

Then they are off to dinner in a dark restaurant with flickering candles dancing saffron beams on snow-white tablecloths; delicate piano music wafts in from the lounge. They clasp hands beneath the table, mutually understanding that this is how it should be and should have been long ago.

Later, he drives her to a vantage point he has checked out before, and together they stand admiring the city's sparkling skyline below, filled with lives that could not be going any better than what he is experiencing right now.

Then he brings her home, and she says it was one of the best nights out she ever had. "Can we do this again sometime?" she asks. A good-night kiss, a promise for another date — he hopes it isn't all a dream that will crumble with the alarm clock banging out the beginning of another day. . . .

How long had I been sitting there? I was crazy. I twisted the key in the ignition, and the radio popped to life in the middle of Tower of Power's "You're Still a Young Man."

I glanced at Janet's place one more time, at the concrete stairs leading to her door, and I made myself a promise:

In the future, I would be able to defy the gravity of my own creation that kept me down in the past. That kept me from her. I had left the way I was and could fling myself out of my limited orbit, to the space between the stars, where anything was possible.

And my first order of business would be to soar up steps like those.

And knock on her door . . . whoever she might be.

The next morning, I avoided stepping on sidewalk cracks as I walked to school. A new hit song on the radio kept playing in my mind: the Cornelius Brothers and Sister Rose's, "Too Late to Turn Back Now."

As I neared Hoover and crossed the street, I didn't see the usual GTOs, Firebirds, Capris, and Camaros in the parking lot. Usually standing around were the same set of guys leaning against their rides, thinking they were too cool to be bothered by the clanging bell warning them to get going to roll room. Sometimes Janet chatted with acquaintances in front of one entrance, so I abruptly changed direction and went to school through a different door.

But today, it was too early for any of that. Besides, the seniors who owned most of those cars were gone. Only a few cars on the road whizzed by; birds still chirped in trees. Instead, I saw Shari standing alone on the stone steps, hugging her books to her chest. And that morning, as she smiled and waved, I noticed the way the early eastern sun touched her, making her hair shine clean and bright as that year's penny.

Maybe not stepping on the cracks paid off.

And maybe everything wasn't as bad as I thought after all.

18.

You can't teach old dogs new tricks, my dad had said. And you couldn't teach them to eat at a variety of restaurants, either. For Brad's graduation dinner, the Inagaki family ended up at the same Japanese restaurant we'd eaten at for little brother Steve's birthday. Instead of sitting at a table, we sat on the bamboo mats in a *tatami* room.

Brad ambushed me right away. "So, what happened to Janet? Or is it that Shari Jennings now?"

The family caught on to that last name.

"Jennings?" Dad said. "Who's this?"

Thanks a lot, Brad!

"Shari Jennings," Brad went on, "a sophomore that I saw Dan a lot with at school."

Steve had to make his presence known. "Dan's got a *girlfrieeend*!"

And my aunt had to contribute. "Sophomore? Kind of young, isn't she?"

"Shari Jennings?" Dad repeated. "Another *hakujin*?"

Mom slapped my father's shoulder. "Dad!"

"What?" Dad responded, then realized how he'd said it. "No! I didn't mean it like that. Two *hakujin* girlfriends would be okay."

I could feel my face flushing.

"She's not quite," Brad said. "Her parents are — what, Dan?"

"Father's *hakujin*, mother's *nisei*," I made known, hoping we could talk about something else.

"Oh, yeah," Dad said, "I know a few like that. Well, good for you, Dan. At least she has a choice — she can go either way, be *hakujin* or *nikkeijin*. Not like us. We're kind of stuck with who we are."

As everybody laughed, including myself, I realized that, only a few months ago, I didn't particularly care for who we were. But then, I learned a few things from Mr. Niles and Mr. Reyes, from Eddie's dad, from Janet, Shari, Davie, Rhonda, Christine, Kathy, and even from Brad. From Jerry, Eddie, and Frank. And from my own parents.

I listened to my family go on about other *sansei,* and listened to them play their version of "The Dozens" — their can-you-top-that comparison game of whose kids were better than whose.

I thought that what my parents and their generation often said and did — and those like Brad who went along with their program — wasn't always their true selves, but more of a role they felt required to play.

Are actors who play bad guys really bad guys?

It's their jobs. And some can feel trapped in that job. Typecast. Janet taught me that.

I sensed someone watching me. I glanced down the table and saw Grandma, eyes smiling at me through her glasses.

My mom said, "*Sansei* are going places we never went, huh?"

"Yeah," Dad agreed, looking at me. "Times have changed. Right, Dan?"

"Yeah . . . they have."

"*Dan-chan.*"

From the other side of the table, Grandma shakily raised her teacup to toast me. My dad helped her raise it all the way.

Dad said, "Okay, I'll drink to that."

Everybody laughed in approval and hoisted their teacups.

The waitress dressed in a kimono stepped into our room — the same waitress from Steve's birthday! She leaned down in front of me, setting down a tray, and I could've peeked at what she wore beneath her kimono. But this time, I made sure I looked away.

As our waitress stepped out of our room and into the hallway, she paused for a second and gave me an approving look.

A look that lingered before she moved on.

She did, didn't she?

I'm sure she did.

DISCOGRAPHY

"Back on the Streets Again," TOWER OF POWER,
East Bay Grease, WEA/Rhino (1970)

"Can I Dedicate," THE LOADING ZONE,
The Loading Zone, Acadia (1968)

"Funky Man," KOOL & THE GANG,
Live at the Sex Machine, Uni/Mercury (1971)

"The Ghetto," DONNY HATHAWAY,
Everything is Everything, WEA/Rhino (1970)

"Inner City Blues," MARVIN GAYE,
What's Going On, Uni/Motown (1971)

"I'll Take You There," THE STAPLE SINGERS,
Be Altitude, Respect Yourself, Fantasy/Stax (1972)

"Outa-Space," BILLY PRESTON,
I Wrote a Simple Song, A&M Records (1971)

"People Make the World Go Round," THE STYLISTICS,
The Stylistics, Amherst (1971)

"Raindrops Keep Falling On My Head," BURT BACHARACH, *Butch Cassidy and the Sundance Kid*, Uni/A&M (1969)

"Suavecito," MALO, *Malo,* WEA/Warner Brothers (1972)

"Theme from Shaft," ISAAC HAYES, *Shaft,* Fantasy/Stax (1971)

"Too Late to Turn Back Now," CORNELIUS BROTHERS AND SISTER ROSE, *Cornelius Brothers and Sister Rose,* United Artists (1972)

"What's Going On," DONNY HATHAWAY, *Live,* Atco (1972)

"What's Going On," MARVIN GAYE, *What's Going On,* Uni/Motown (1971)

"You Are Everything," THE STYLISTICS, *The Stylistics,* Amherst (1971)

"You're Still a Young Man," TOWER OF POWER, *Bump City,* WEA/Warner Brothers (1972)

"You've Got a Friend," ROBERTA FLACK & DONNY HATHAWAY, Atlantic (1972)

"Valdez in the Country," COLD BLOOD, *First Taste of Sin,* Warner Bros. Records Inc. (1972)

DATE DUE
